THE SUGAR CUBE IN THE SKY

THE SUGAR CUBE
IN THE SKY

Stephen Debenham

The Book Guild Ltd
Sussex, England

The Book Guild Limited
25 High Street
Lewes, Sussex

First published 1989
© Stephen Debenham 1989

Set in Linotron Cartier

Typeset by Book Economy Services

Printed in Great Britain by
Antony Rowe Ltd
Chippenham

ISBN 0 86332 414 2

Prologue

Mutterings could be heard in the side passage running alongside Stephen Baxter's house. Several years have now passed. The pound is worth but a few pennies, new stars and galaxies have been discovered, there are over 1000 million people in China, and Uganda is likely to win the next World Cup. Even the offer of a free tea service to win your bank account, or a free burial service when you purchase some company shares are but fleeting notions and promises, soon forgotten by a sated public bewildered and finally bored by the sheer volume of choice.

Two dustmen, one middle aged, and the other a teenager, have made a discovery in the rubbish bin. A few days ago Stephen had been clearing out an old wardrobe and had come across several rolls of 'Big 10' trading stamps languishing among some fading T shirts. His wife threw them out without a second thought. The older man was now picking up the rolls in the manner of an old prospector making his first gold strike after years of failure. His young associate merely stared back at him nonplussed. He didn't recognise the green rolls which had had such effect on his mate, and so could not comprehend the impact and emotion the curled up sticky paper could once command. It didn't matter. They were quite worthless now anyway and the euphoria which had so gripped his companion evaporated. What happened, who made the stamps and how it all had vanished so quickly were forgotten issues.

The older man shrugged his shoulders, smiled and tossed aside their would-be bounty. They picked up their gloves and went about their business. . . .

1

From his newly acquired and pristine office Baxter surveyed the realm of the Empire that had just taken him under its wing. Through the twelfth floor window he wondered at the sight of brand-new saloon cars throbbing in and out from under the giant Sugar Cube which had, in the short space of a few years, become the nerve centre of the country's fastest growing and most successful phenomenon, The Green Dragon Trading Stamp Company.

The battle fleet lay before him as far off as he could see, newly acquired lines of automobiles gleaming in the sun. Little blue Escorts for the pioneer reps, larger Cortinas for the service reps, Ford Granadas for the multiple men and managers and a host of trucks, articulated lorries and vans in the now nationally familiar livery of black and orange on a solid green background. A special compound contained the Mercedes, Jaguars and Bentleys which were the playthings of the new gods who reigned from the thirteenth floor.

The surge of activity going on down below mesmerised him. He started suddenly and swung round, worried that someone would burst in and find him daydreaming. Nothing, no-one stirred, everything was quiet. He continued to view the brightly patterned hubbub below. The Sugar Cube seemed an apt description of the building. Its location on the apex of the High Street gave it an absolute prominence unmatched by anything else on the local skyline, and from either end of the town the silvery slab appeared to be set high upon a plinth on account of a structured indentation ten feet above ground level. In Saxon times one would have spoken of an ideal defensive site. Who could predict that the absence of turrets, draw-bridge, and moat would seem more a psychological omission, given the sort of siege mentality the Company would develop in the times ahead. Another feature was aesthetic rather than strategic. Like Ayers Rock in the Australian desert, the edifice had a chameleon capacity somehow to shift its hue from the uniform concrete grey to white in the bright sunlight. This was due not to any magical capacity bestowed upon the architecture but purely the result of a reflection from an abandoned chemical warehouse, the enormous white roof of which lit up two sides of the Cube. All this was of great value to the one-time visitor in a car or cab; HQ was visible for miles. To the inmate of its upper reaches, however, there was a sense of isolation and exposed vulnerability, due in no small measure to the acreage of the parking area which prevented any other building from interrupting the view. Baxter imagined himself perched on the tower of an aircraft-carrier, facing an empty sea. Up above him, the creators of this new Empire were safely sealed off from the ants at the bottom by dint of several notices and warnings informing all and sundry that the twelfth floor was the top level and voyages beyond that point would not be welcomed. The contrast, as Baxter would soon discover, was as marked as a tourist would find crossing from East to West Berlin, or a cruise passenger suddenly finding himself in first class after several days in the galley.

Down below, the hordes now sustaining their newly found lifestyle were engaged in a multitude of specially created functions designed to ensure the smooth running of this weird and wonderful enterprise. Baxter contemplated an unknown and uncharted future.

The circumstances behind his recent arrival were not particularly unusual. As a young business graduate, he had never consciously thought about the Company from a job viewpoint. He had been a competitor in one of Green Dragon's sponsored tennis tournaments during the sumer, and had inadvertantly strayed into the hospitality tent, which he took for a hastily constructed changing room. A glass had been thrust into his hand and before he knew what was happening he was engaged in earnest conversation with the Merchandise Director. He told Baxter an enthralling story with missionary zeal. The facts tumbled out of his mouth at an unerring rate. 4,000 employees in the space of 6 years, a turnover of £52 million, 300 cars, 35 gift houses, an executive jet, sports and social club, and so on and so forth. It was all powerful medicine reinforced by unlimited paper mugs of sparkling wine. The tent itself was groaning with food and drink and Baxter found himself easily seduced by the heady atmosphere. If the Company could entertain in this sort of style there surely must be a dynamic management team and a strong balance sheet. The idea of being part of this exciting world suddenly took root and he wondered if he could broach the subject to his host. By the time he was ready to ask such a question he had been presented with a fait accompli. He was offered a position as a marketing executive at head office. All Baxter remembered in retrospect before leaving the tent in the evening was signing a form and disappearing with a makeshift employment letter in one hand and a sports bag in the other.

A soft distant ringing tone penetrated Baxter's trance. It came from a battery of telephones in the deserted outer office. Perhaps now someone would appear out of the void and pick it up. The bell purred away unattended. No sign of life anywhere. He watched and waited. Whoever was on the other end was not giving up. He could stand it no longer. Finding a battery of telephones he picked up one of the receivers.

'Mr Baxter, this is Gillian, Rupert Bugbear's secretary. RB apologises for neglecting you so since your arrival. He's been very busy. Could you come up and see him at 2.00?'

He replaced the receiver. The isolation and quietness of the past few days were put behind him now that a definite appointment had been made. Now, at last, he would be given some outline of what would be required of him and from no less than the Managing Director himself. The prospect was exciting yet daunting; a briefing from the man who had liked the early ideas of the Founder of Green Dragon and so had agreed to direct the new company's fortunes during the great man's frequent absences.

Baxter walked back into his office feeling distinctly vulnerable, realising that he knew very little about the kind of business which he had been employed to help flourish. With a few hours to kill it seemed a good idea to cram in a few facts about his new employers before the meeting with RB. He wandered out of his room, down the deserted corridors looking for inspiration. The third door along provided the answer. It was marked 'Information Library'. Perfect. Just what he wanted. Things were definitely looking up. He coughed, paused, and went in. He was alone no longer.

A tall gangling youth was lolling by an open window in the corner. From where Baxter was standing the boy appeared to be grasping handfuls of pink confetti and dropping them into the void below. He was gazing blankly at the sky and appeared almost half asleep. Baxter

9

coughed again and introduced himself. The boy suddenly came alive, slammed the window and came across the room.

'Hello, I'm Peter Truckley – like a coffee?' It wasn't long before the youngster had given his new colleague a potted history of his short and rather unfortunate introduction to the world of trading stamps. Apparently this was his first job after having dropped out of college notwithstanding dozens of interviews with prospective companies, all of which he'd managed to muff ignominiously. Green Dragon went against the grain and accepted him. Peter thought his luck had changed, but a few weeks later everything had gone sour. Disaster struck on the very first mission he was entrusted with. Assuming the guise of a normal shopper he was asked to note down prices of goods in stores giving the rival Pink or Blue stamps. The monitoring would have to be done surreptitiously and cover a check list of 30 everyday food items. Not a difficult mission for someone of moderate intelligence. Peter, however, decided on a way of doing this which more experienced infiltrators would have avoided. Instead of scribbling down little notes on a pad, he took a dictaphone into Granline Stores, and was immediately apprehended on close circuit television changing the tapes. Escorted out by the store detective it was not long before all the top brass of Green Dragon were told and the Marketing department were humiliated before the rest of the Company. In the manner of a discredited spy, Truckley was soon entrusted with nothing more adventurous than seeing how fast the average stamp saver would fill a 48 page saver book given the average amount of saliva. Not unnaturally disillusionment for Peter set in pretty fast. He had become an unperson in the space of a few months.

Baxter listened to his story sympathetically and apprehensively as the consequences of the price of failure slowly dawned on him.

He now realised that he could well be asked by RB to embark upon a parallel exercise and suffer a similar fate. With this disturbing thought at the back of his mind he remembered the reason for his coming into the library. He grabbed a huge manual labelled 'All you need to know about Trading Stamps' and made for the door. As he said goodbye to Peter, it was now clear what Truckley had been doing when he came in. What Baxter took for confetti were in fact Pink competitor stamps which the bored and frustrated youngster had wantonly shovelled out of the window onto the oil stained tarmac of the rear entrance of the building. Baxter quickly assumed Peter must now have a kind of death wish and was looking to be shown the door. Even if people on lower floors missed the pink snowstorm passing by them, the pile on the tarmac where RB made his daily entrance could hardly be missed.

All his attention now centred on the very short walk down the corridor, up the carpeted stairs, past the warning notices towards the MD's office. He was a lot less confident about things since he chanced upon the library and cursed himself for even going in. Still, it was too late now to worry about that. He straightened his tie, made sure he had a pen and notebook, and looked around for an indication as to the whereabouts of Bugbear's office.

Once up on the top level it took him only a few seconds to realise that just about everything around him were in varying shades of the same colour – green. The carpets were sage, desks and cabinets emerald, and the wallpaper and ceiling dark olive punctuated with recessed spotlights. The overall effect was surprisingly pleasant and actually quite tasteful.

Although it was necessary that the Board were obliged to reflect the Company image by choosing the right colours to decorate its inner sanctum, someone had nevertheless made sure that the gaudy green and orange which adorned the gift houses and client shops were noticeably absent here. Haseys, the advertising agency chosen by its former employee, Warren Clews, had rightly tried to differentiate between the way the public saw Green Dragon as overtly bold and brash, and the portrayal offered to VIP clients coming upstairs for the first time – a serenely elegant and subdued display of good taste. The directors themselves, many of whom had suddenly jumped from being milkmen, car salesmen or bookmakers to the top deck, were quite blind to this subtlety. Their judgement on matters cultural or artistic were thankfully never called upon. Two of them, Warren Clews and Ian Hersey, had tried to leave when it seemed the whole stamp idea would peter out and Green Dragon with it. Rejected by their former employers, United Dairies and Ladbrookes, they seemed certainties for an early return to the dole queue. Out of the blue the Boshko account arrived and their inability to leave became a God-given blessing as the money rolled in and the tide swept them upstairs into the beautiful green surroundings now casting their spell on Stephen Baxter.

One more ante-room and past Gillian, Bugbear's secretary, and there he was, in the holy of holies. The room must have been at least 40 feet long. The wall a mass of photographs and diplomas dedicated to the highlights of RB's career. The heavy aroma of cigar smoke fought with the scent of creeper and rubber plants for dominance.

The squat tubby figure swung round and faced him. So large was his desk and so wide that the two men had difficulty in achieving a handshake. The awkward introduction over, RB gave his rather overawed companion some insight into the stunning growth of the Company. It all started in the 1950s, when the Founder, then a part owner of a couple of ironmongers, visited the USA. He became highly impressed by that nation's adoption of the trading stamp as an incentive for the consumer to buy products ranging from saucepans to luxury yachts. He returned in 1958 and together with two old cronies established the embryo from which the current company had grown into the mighty empire known all over the land. The Founder hired a team of young men to approach garages and stores and put to their proprietors a proposition:- 'Give stamps with your product and it will triple turnover in under a year'. 'This was no empty promise', affirmed RB, 'Look all around you – it really does produce all this'. The sale of stamp pads to retailers with the option to give double, triple or four times the normal allocation back to the customer was the magic yet proven formula.

After a 20-minute talk, Baxter felt obliged to say something.

'Suppose,' he said 'A shopkeeper had spent a fortune buying pads from our salesmen, having signed an agreement, and still found, even after offering multiple amounts the goods weren't sold at the rate to make it worthwhile.'

There was a long silence. It wasn't an unreasonable question. A fundamental query to the whole argument surely. Baxter knew he'd overreached himself – he was challenging the architect on the safety of his design. It was like asking the Pope whether he believed in God! These were the only words he had uttered apart from the 'Good afternoon' when he came in. His debut could become as disastrous as Peters! RB's greasy leer turned sour. The need to reply however forced the Managing Director into an involuntary smile. The tension had to find an outlet somewhere nonetheless. He stood up and, slowly pacing the floor, systematically ground the many golf balls which were scattered over the carpet, deep into the pile.

'No-one asks these sort of questions – not on our side anyway. The only way that would happen would be if the owner was totally incompetent with his pricing, and if that were the case he may as well close down.'

Of course, this is what frequently did occur, especially with small uncompetitive outlets in poor locations. The cost of buying the stamps hastened the quick road to bankruptcy. Green Dragon, in the person of RB and his junior crusaders, did everything in their power to keep the outlet going, sometimes offering stamp pads at rock bottom prices. The last thing the Company wanted was for any disgruntled retailer to blabber off to the local paper that stamps had caused his downfall. This situation called for the utmost diplomacy which few persons in the Sugar Cube were able to provide. All too often the poor shop-keeper was 'bought off' in many different guises, and if he were really on his knees he would ultimately be given a job. The huge warehouse the Company owned at Coventry employed well over 100 people – 3 of them were failed proprietors who were now helping to sustain the system which had caused their downfall.

Baxter felt he should change his tack. 'And to think, sir' he said, 'the entire operation – stamps, gift shops, warehousing, jobs, people – all controlled from this very room.' The remark had the desired effect. RB smiled again. As Baxter would discover in the future any blunder, whether actual or implied, could be remedied by flattery. A warm glow seemed to come over the crow's-nest in the sky.

'Quite right. Quite right,' said RB, 'not only that, but look around you, as far as you can see – restaurants, hairdressers, sandwich bars – you name it, all dependent on us one way or another. Look for yourself.'

RB got up, put his arm around Baxter and led him to the window. Unfortunately a thick mist had encapsulated the top of the building, including the thirteenth level. Nobody could see anything. Bugbear shrugged his shoulders and they both sat down again. The brief era of good feeling had melted away. RB was down to business. Baxter would need to attend a short training course and then be prepared for his first real mission, ostensibly a photographic surveillance exercise on behalf of Sir Stamford Brook, president of Boshko Stores, Green Dragon's biggest client. Although the company had many hundreds of accounts of varying sizes, Boshko was by far the largest and a linchpin of the Founder's empire.

Baxter was amazed that he should be entrusted with such a job scarcely a week after his arrival. His disastrous blooding of Peter Truckley surely would have made RB wary of delegating such a brief to someone as green and untried as himself. The consequences of the outcome would be far-reaching.

Granline Stores, Boshko's main rival were opening a new outlet in Scotland, giving away pink stamps. The success of this launch would block any chance Green Dragon would have of penetrating the north, an area they had not managed to swamp to the same degree as the rest of the land. Furthermore it would also damage Boshko who had plans to move into the same area using green.

RB grimaced, thumped the table and looked down at Baxter.

'I want this to be the most calamitous introduction they've ever had north of the border. Make sure it's a failure' he snapped.

Baxter winced. Secretly noting down prices or taking photographs of floor layouts was one thing. Sabotage was way out of line. Before he had a chance to voice any objections RB came in again. 'How you do it doesn't matter. There's bound to be an opening ceremony performed by some minor celebrity. We do the same things with Stamford. Stephen, there are dozens of ways of spoiling the day. Jam up the High Street, confuse the customers with fire warnings, unplug the microphone – you'll find something.' 'By myself?' enquired the agent apparent. 'Certainly,' asserted RB. 'We can't have too many of us up there or they'd soon smell a rat.'

Baxter sat open mouthed, unable to comprehend what was being drilled into him. RB tempered the tone down a bit.

'Don't set fire to the place or anything like that. Remember we don't want the locals so antagonised that they get the Council to prohibit any more intrusions. All we need to do is to make very plain that Granline are an incompetent bunch of idiots, and how much better it would be if someone else had started up instead of them. Then I'll send up Truston and his team.'

'How will that help?' quizzed Baxter.

'They'll get to know everyone who matters in town. We start off with a few parties in the top hotels and make sure raffle prizes are won by the mayor, councillors and local traders. Before long we can have Vivienne and her personality girls giving away stamps in the High Street. Once they get a taste for green, the most influential local businessman, following a free trip to the States or Europe, will write to the *Chronicle* suggesting Boshko move in giving green. By that time we'll have a site for a gift house plus a store. Granline will be swamped and we should be able to kill them off up there once and for all.'

RB paused and waited for Stephen to say something. The latter remained silent, reconciled to the task. 'Come up with something Stephen. This is a chance to put yourself on the map. Matt Pearson reckoned you had something which is why we hired you. Learn a bit about the business and then get up there.'

Baxter, in the manner of a courtier who had overstayed his presence in the King's company, sensed that it was time for him to leave. No more orders or directions were coming from the far side of the table. He picked up his green notebook and pen, half bowed and made for the door.

Laurie Rabbler burst in clutching a piece of paper and as usual urgency was written all over his face. Sixtyish, distinguished, and the kind of senior executive Green Dragon saw as an ideal antidote to the flashy mohair-suited salesman who personified the bulk of the Company, Laurie had become Bugbear's personal aide-de-camp. Because of his smart bank-manager appearance he spent a good deal of time at weekends with the photographer of the house magazine, presenting cups to the winners of tennis and swimming competitions sponsored by the Company. No edition of 'G/D News' would be without his beaming avuncular smile. Perhaps his prize-giving function, which he performed exceedingly well, in some way made up for his performance in the working week, since no-one ever discovered the purpose behind his constant state of blinding panic which seemed to attend his every move. Each job that Laurie was currently engaged upon was written on a single sheet of paper which never left his hand from his morning entrance to his late night departure. No-one ever saw what the paper contained and Laurie never looked at it himself, it was just a safety first standby in case he forgot where he was going, and a justification for being in such a hurry. The four sides of the Sugar Cube would echo to his frantic speed about the floor which would often have dire consequences when crashing into the tea trolley ladies on a 90-degree turn.

The three men just looked at each other as RB prepared to deal with Laurie for the umpteenth time that day. He smiled as he dismissed Baxter: 'You'll love it here Stephen, its just like living.'

Baxter went back down to his office, still considering his awesome brief and RB's parting words. It was well past 4 o'clock, the mist had cleared, and through his open door he caught sight of Peter Truckley once more, as he had left him in the library only this time fast asleep in a chair. He had positioned himself in such a way that by opening the window a few inches, the late afternoon sun had hit him full face. As time had progressed he had moved around so as never to be out of the sun. The exertion must have taken its toll for he dozed soundly.

Back in his own quarter he watched the last of the cars returning to the compound for the evening, all the crusaders safely back to base to fight another day.

He was aware of a strange whining noise, an intrusion he certainly hadn't experienced earlier in the day when silence reigned in his own territory. The hum seemed to be coming from the top of the window. He opened it and peered outside. A gigantic illuminated 'E' was buzzing over his head; part of the Company name to dominate the night sky. He wondered what life under the 'E' was going to be like. He would soon find out.

2

For Stephen, it was certainly a strange beginning in a brave new world. Though unprepared and ill-equipped to cope with his new role, still he was not alone. Millions were coming to terms with the transition from the 50s to the 60s. The Jurassic to the Devonian. Feathers replaced by scales. Words, concepts, practices, which left the uncalibrated punter stranded and lost whilst offering wonderful opportunities for those able to grasp the new ideas. The word 'marketing' had drifted over the ocean from the Harvard Business School and left in its wake a rapidly evolving series of indispensable functions. The component parts and by-words of the new science – the 'product life cycle', the Z chart, ink blot tests and dichotomous questioning. Attenuated responses were declared out of fashion as 'no' gave way to 'negative' and 'yes' to 'affirmative'. Public relations did not mean putting uncle in a shop window or displaying granny on a 48-sheet poster – it now had an official edict, 'the sustained effort to establish and maintain mutual understanding between an organisation and its publics'. Elsewhere, customs were shifting and treading new ground, some were ephemeral and faddish but as several gained a foothold and trends became ensconced the old order was gradually but permanently obliterated by the new. Butlin's gave way first to the Costa Brava and then Greece; motor cars and records got smaller and so did clothing – the mini car, mini skirt and the 45 rpm disc. Single records sold in the 60s in a way unparalleled before or since. The man in the street became a 'consumer' for the first time and a most important target for new entrepreneurs ready, willing, and (aided by an investigative method dubbed 'market research') able to cash in on whatever vocabulary was exploitable. Most significantly, in view of the still undreamt-of fuel crisis, power strikes and market crash of the mid-70s, jobs were plentiful and very often could materialise through the chanciest circumstance or improbable meeting. Nowhere was this more apparent than in the rapidly expanding television and advertising sectors. The writings of Marshall McLuhan and Vance Packard emphasised that consumer sovereignty was a myth and that given suitable 'back up' every idea could be made to develop a silver lining. The television commercial, with its catchy music (now termed a 'jingle'), made covetousness an acceptable trait and if by the standards of the 80s the washing machines and automobiles resembled tanks and dinosaurs, the eager viewer had not yet reached the state of bored cynicism universally present some twenty years later. Curiosity and wonderment gave way to a mood of positive acquisitiveness – the squirrel instinct – and thus in this way a company sprang up offering a rainbow at the end of that most repetitive of duties, the shopping expedition. Even the male population, always reluctant to share this chore, could be persuaded to double his petrol consumption or push a trolley around a supermarket if, at the end of a month or a year, a set of golf clubs came 'absolutely free' from the Green Dragon showroom.

In the stores themselves a revolution had taken place, bringing them up to date with the situation in America a decade earlier. Food was purer, fresher and more hygienic; canning was supplanted in instances by freezing and drying to produce the 'convenience' food. The rapid demise of the corner shop put an abrupt end to personal service and advice. The self-service store displayed goods which could call on no support from the proprietor. The product would have to stand on its own merits, and in turn the food giants would be obliged to depend upon the chemical industry for new containers, packs and materials so as to steal a march on the opposition.

So the shackles of the 50s fell off as the expectations of Galbraith's 'Affluent Society' came to fruition. The scene was set for the Company of the decade and those who would be running it.

David Martin was the classic embodiment of the shining Green Dragon crusader. A bright breezy former insurance salesman and part-time bingo caller, he had gratefully allowed himself to be swept up in the euphoria which gripped those working in the early growth years of the Company. Now after five years of pioneering, service and multiple selling, his status had risen from a bang on the door 'Good morning Mr Retailer' first timer, to a respectable Empire smoothie, well known to the Board of Directors, who had all been through the same school.

It was not unreasonable therefore to suppose that with such a background Martin would have been alive to the sort of practises he himself employed and admired. Not so. Straddled on the northbound carriageway of the M1 motorway in fading light the distraught driver contemplated his tin dinosaur gently expiring in a haze of smoke. Designed to hitching his way out of trouble Martin suddenly beheld the vision of a pick up truck which appeared from out of nowhere. Instant salvation. Two men in peaked caps jumped down, smiled at the relieved executive and then proceeded to winch the moribund vehicle aboard their truck. Within five minutes the stricken car had been loaded and as the rescuers slipped off into the gloaming with their prize Martin glanced at the legend on the tailboard – Complete Overhauls Now. The implication of the initials lost on its victim.

Back at head office the unexpected loss of another company car to motorway con-men caused little stir. Hardly a day seemed to go by without some form of depletion to the enormous fleet. The Transport Manager treated his machines as if they were fighters' planes during the Battle of Britain; some would be lost, many would be damaged, and several would disappear for a few days then re-appear in a different place on the tarmac.

Perhaps it was because the fleet had grown at such an exponential rate that proper custody of cars seemed out of control from the very beginning. The merchandise directors refusal to pass up any deal offered by Ford meant the arrival of fresh batches of unassigned vehicles to swell the parking lot. An enterprising soul would have set up a satellite shuttle from the outer limits to the Cube itself as a serious proposition. Then there was the Transport Manager himself – the original old woman in the shoe; cars instead of children; a man bemused, besieged and completely overwhelmed.

Baxter was allocated a pool car as were all non-managers of his ilk. For this particular assignment he was conscious of acquiring a vehicle completely devoid of any markings or tell-tale clues which could be traced back to the Company. The disruption which he had been instructed to cause at Granline's new store must be seen to be as accidental as possible. The perpetrators would vanish in the Highland mist, the proprietors never to suspect a pre-emptive strike plotted 400 miles south. It was a naive assumption but one they had to work towards. Doubtless open warfare would break out soon enough, but for the time being both sides contented themselves with hit and run guerilla tactics.

The agent apparent now determined to make his way down to the Transport Department on the first floor. That it should take him so long was due to a poor choice of day for a safari downstairs. It so happened the Transport Department shared the whole of the first floor with the canteen, and on each Friday afternoon at the end of the month the restaurant was cleared for a Green Dragon staff sale. Communications and general movement were very difficult. A sense of excitement built up during the morning, and the four liftmen braced themselves for their most disagreeable shift of the working year. The consequences of the sale were that both lifts were unobtainable all afternoon for normal business, as elevator and stairway were jammed with managers and tea ladies all humping radios, tables, bicycles and jewellery this way or that. These Friday jamborees paralysed the in-house services to such an extent that anyone wanting personnel advice or photocopying would abandon their plan 'till Monday morning. Everything apparently warranted the pandemonium that accompanied the event however, since for a few pounds typists and van drivers could pick up still functioning damaged gift house items or surpluses caused by over-stocking.

Baxter thumped the lift button, alive to the din wafting from below decks, but still unaware of the reason. He gave up and started to walk down the main staircase. One flight down on the eleventh, a one-way slanging match was in progress between Douglas Alcott the Publicity Manager, and one of the liftmen. Alcott had purloined a bicycle in the sale and wantonly flouting his authority had requisitioned an elevator for his exclusive use to get the machine upstairs. Attempting to get it out again on the eleventh, he somehow got it jammed across the door and the green attendant was taking heavy abuse when Stephen arrived on the scene. The presence of a third party interrupted Douglas's flow as Baxter ignored them and studied the problem. The only way to release the bike and doors would be to kick the machine back inside the lift and try again. He consulted the two adversaries who, having no inspiration of their own, readily agreed to his plan. Stephen took a running leap at the bike with disastrous results. The machine snapped in two, and as both parts fell into the lift, the doors slammed shut and the lift plummeted to earth in answer to a call from the beleagered first floor. Alcott was livid. Five minutes earlier he was the proud possessor of a new bicycle, the two pieces of which were now being squashed and trodden over by the crazed bargain-hunters cramming into the lift below. He glared hard at the others and then proceeded to walk down with as much dignity as the situation would allow. Not a very good introduction to a key character in the Company, thought Stephen.

So grateful was the lift-man for his deliverance from DNA that he offered to take Baxter direct to the first floor, ignoring the cries and shouts of the sales revellers in between. Before disembarking the distraught retainer gave his rescuer a little insight into his problems. Clearly starved of any prolonged conversation (since maximum journey times are less than two minutes) Baxter was a captive audience and his new ally was not going to let him off lightly.

When the Company first took up lodging in the Sugar Cube they only occupied three floors and two lifts were adequate for both persons and goods. As the business grew the volume of internal traffic intensified and overnight the lot of the lift men became unenviable. The builders never even bothered to instal a goods lift, for even the most enthusiastic stamp crusader could never have visualised the speed at which the idea took off. Listening to this tale Baxter felt decidedly claustrophobic. Despite reaching first floor level, the unhappy saga dragged on and it was at this point that he was aware of size and area. The two of them filled half the floor space. He now understood the cause of frustration and bad blood. Since one operator represented a quarter of the machines carrying capacity, allied to the rule that attendant-less trips were forbidden, it was hardly surprising that anyone waiting on a lower floor for a trip to the gods was bound to be disappointed.

He finally emerged in the enormous transport room. It was functional and basic. Log books, service manuals and keys on the metal desks; fast cars, girls and football teams on the walls. It seemed distinctly undermanned, and Baxter had no trouble in spotting Dan Farsons, the manager. The sort of authority which the latter asserted was shown up by the fact that almost all his helpers had abandoned their posts to join the sales stampede next door. The prospects were not encouraging for much co-operation, thought Stephen. His suspicions were confirmed when, at the end of a lucid explanation of his needs, the Transport Manager silently tossed him a bunch of keys with a tab including the registration number. Farsons, unintelligible to all, including perhaps his own family, lifted his arms towards the window and muttered something which Baxter interpreted as meaning the far end of the park.

Once on the tarmac and at ground level, finding his quarry was a real challenge. There were thousands of cars and nearly all were identical. So crammed together was the fleet that merely reading the number plates was a job in itself. If only Farsons had mentioned a colour it might have been a start. Surely an old banger would stick out amongst these 'dinky toys'. Ten minutes became twenty as he scanned the number plates in vain. He toyed with the idea of going back to Farsons and seeing whether he could induce him to be more helpful. Naive though he still was about the Company, Baxter rightly assumed it would take more than polite charm to get any co-operation, in time he would come to know how much it took to get the help he needed.

He pressed on with crouched head and shoulders, and on finding a possible candidate got down on all fours for a closer look. He felt a tap on his head. Three burly security guards were standing over him. Because of the high loss of vehicles uniformed guards were briefed to keep a day and night watch on the compound, training their binoculars from their sixth floor base. As several genuine thieves were picked up in broad daylight, trying doors and peering through windscreens, he was naturally taken for one. The ensuing embarrass-ment of being frog-marched back into your own building brought red faces to all concerned. Identifications established, the wrong was soon righted however, and back outside the elusive saloon located. As a car it was everything the others were not. Baxter wondered how he came to have so much trouble finding it in the first place. A dirty maroon sedan, it languished under a bush, liberally covered in pigeon droppings and catkins. By no stretch of the imagination could this be deemed a tool of any company. As far as his present needs ran, it looked just right. He seemed satisfied and felt things were falling into place. The pieces of the equation were starting to fit together. Now it was time to go and find out about trading stamps.

His next stop was, therefore, the training room. Baxter attended the class for a week but new salesmen who had just been hired were required to stay two full weeks. The sessions took the uninitiated through all the mechanics of stamp trading, stamp arithmetic, the background of the Company, overcoming objections by reluctant retailers and, of course, the ultimate prize of getting the shopkeepers signature on the franchise agreement, thus closing the sale.

The applicants came from every trade or business one could imagine but, like a recruit to the Foreign Legion, were joining up because somewhere along the line things had not worked out the way they had planned. Mechanics, bookeepers and life insurance salesmen all fell in line for the Monday morning roll call. Several would drop out after the first week but over half would stay the course. It was the head-to-head encounter with the prospect that most of the pioneer crusaders found the most daunting ordeal. It was safely impressed on them in the training room that their Sales Manual covered just about any question or objection that was likely to be raised by the shopkeeper or store manager.

In theory then, all they had to do was to learn the correct counter to whatever verbal challenge was posed and they would be alright. In the field, as one might expect, the realities were a little different. Certain salesmen, fresh from the course, had in fact panicked when confronted with the manager of a shop contemplating the Green Dragon plan. Most of them had scant ability to deal with relevant points outside the rehearsed arguments. For example, a point would arise whereby the prospect was getting a trifle fed up with the persistence of the salesman.

'Once you start stamps you're always on the hook, you can't stop'. The salesman's response: 'When you're making money at this rate you won't want to stop.' Quite often when the banter had exceeded several exchanges and the retailer was being pestered by other customers, he quickly lost his patience and then the flack would really start to fly.

All this, however, was way off in the future; right now the pioneers were quite happy merely to finish the course. Of one thing there was no doubt, the survivors of the two-week trial certainly felt they had achieved something, and it was hard to deny that this was so. Before they had started many were unemployed or only eking out a living, and now although their new salary was not much, they had a spanking new car, a glistening smile, at least a month's worth of security, a feeling of belonging and a book full of contracts ready to be signed. These then were the pioneers who would blaze a trail across the country, spreading the stamp gospel in uncharted territories. Their hope was that once they had broken down a few retailers, and after a period of up to 18 months they would graduate to service reps. This latter being would carry no contracts, solely boxes of stamp pads, to replenish diminishing stocks. His salary was higher, and the cc of his car greater (for motor status was of great import within the Empire) though the envied bonus commission factor no longer applied.

3

The week passed very quickly for Stephen, and he carried back an enormous batch of material lavished on him by the Training Officer. Everything he amassed was fine and dandy for the aspiring pioneer, but not very much good for an apprentice saboteur. He put aside the Training Manual and concentrated on a silver metallic box which had been left on the desk during his week away. It contained the camera for his mission, and also a special mount so that he could attach it to the door of his car. A cable release, autowinder and tiny pair of binoculars completed the outfit. All very necessary for the job in hand. He was anxious to become completely familiar with the equipment before going north, as Bugbear had scribbled a memo to the effect that a photo record of everything Stephen considered important would also be required.

Baxter took the camera out of the box, loaded a film, and generally got the feel of it. It felt a good deal heavier than anything he had handled before, though on first inspection he could not understand why. It was definitely top heavy, and most certainly not the sort of device to meet the requirements of what lay before him. There was no question of any fast takes with this thing; it was as much as he could do merely to hold it steady in the comfort of his own office, let alone clandestinely along some windswept Scottish street. The makers name was on the base plate – Zeiss GDR. Built like their tanks and tractors; robust, indestructible and full of rivets.

The moment he looked through the viewfinder something seemed very wrong. He couldn't focus on anything. Moving over to the window however was a different story. Whoever had supplied the camera had fitted a mini-telephoto instead of the standard 50mm lens. This explained its great weight and the blur when he tried focusing close up on the desk. Now it fell into place. The car mount was no optional extra, it was a prime requisite. He could now appreciate the potential of this camera. It would be quite possible to sit in a parked vehicle a couple of hundred yards away and capture all the highlights of the Granline opening. Stephen was eager to try out his new toy. Using the car clamp he fixed the camera on the metal surround of the open window and wound the film round until a number 1 registered in the frame counter. He cocked the lever and everything was set.

The range of options was quite extensive. Such was the view from the twelfth floor that he could pick out almost anything that took his fancy. The clock tower beyond the car park, station, and library was a good half-mile away so Stephen focused on the blue and gold clock face. He could virtually see the gold hands move over the roman numerals, such was the power of the lens.

He decided to come in a bit as he confidently expected the subject matter in Scotland would be a lot closer than that. He tilted the camera downwards. The range was now about 400 yards at the point where the vast car park ended and a slip road led out into the main High Street. Coaxing the focusing gently round, the gates at the end of the compound were clear and sharp. Just into the bottom right corner of the frame Stephen caught sight of a hand and arm quite still. He took his eyes away from the viewfinder and adjusted the axis. A grey suited figure came slap bang into view with his back to camera. The appearance was familiar but unless the figure turned sideways to show profile he could not make a positive identification. Baxter backed away from the camera and rummaged through the metallic box for the binoculars. He felt like a roof top assassin identifying his prey. The figure had now turned sideways and the face occupied the full frame of the field glasses – Douglas Alcott.

Neither hunter or hunted changed their position. Stephen kept the glasses firmly fixed on the target. What on earth was he waiting for? Strangely enough it was noticeable that if, and presuming Alcott was waiting for a lift, he was consistently facing the least likely direction for one to come. Stephen moved the glasses away from Alcott towards the direction which was obviously occupying his attention. The slip road vanished behind a clump of pine trees. It didn't seem to lead to anything. Back to the Publicity Manager who maintained his gaze unerringly, punctuated with quick glances at his watch. All of a sudden a large black limousine punched its way through the pine trees and in a matter of seconds had pulled up alongside Alcott. Baxter switched to the pre-set telephoto and the autowinder did its bit. He reverted to the binoculars once more and followed it into the High Street. There was a chauffeur driving and Alcott had clearly joined the one other person in the back seat. The car was easily identified as a 1965 Cadillac. Stephen tried to read the messge above the number plate but could only make out the letters ILL before a bus got in the way and the quarry was gone for good.

It had been a fascinating ten minutes and he had been totally absorbed. He felt a surge of excitement and anticipation as he wondered how this little 'dummy run' would compare with the real thing he was about to embark upon. Harmlessly spying on a member of staff from such an ideal viewing platform was one thing, doing it in alien territory quite another.

Satisfied with his experiment Stephen packed the equipment away, not in the least bit aware his practice session just ended might well have been worth a little closer scrutiny.

Voices were becoming increasingly audible through the thin walls of his office. It was Dan Turpin in full flood. Whoever was at the other end of the phone was getting it loud and clear. The tone was one of exasperation and annoyance.

'Everytime I go upstairs I seem to get bombarded with panic reports on fresh hypermarket openings or some new promotion Pink are giving to worry us. Any unfamiliar shop sign or banner seems to suggest that the business in question is going to knock us for six overnight. We are painfully over-examining everything and fastidiously delving into non-existent threats. Red alert status is being given to the most trivial and obscure competitive move.'

Dan promptly went silent. His listener took over and it was several minutes before Turpin was able to resume his theme.

'Yes of course we've got to run them all to ground, but within reason for God's sake. I'm telling you it's absurd. We're so far ahead of Pink it's ridiculous. Look, I worship the green god as much as you do but instead of this waste of energy shouldn't we be signing up for the new ones, not constantly looking over the shoulder at Pinkerton's boys? Even we don't have unlimited resources.'

Stephen pressed his ear closer to the wall, curious to identify Dan's sparring partner. The clatter of tea cups in the passage didn't help. The silence was a lot longer this time, perhaps Dan was running into some stiff opposition.

'When he gets back it won't be long before he wants to know what projects are on the go. Trouble is there'll be no-one here to tell him. Everyone who matters is probably surreptitiously hiding in a car outside some innocuous grocer, armed with a camera, a notebook, and after they've been sitting there for hours, a stiff neck. Honestly Laurie this hysteria is like a contagious disease – it's becoming more rampant every day. . . .'

The conversation started to tail off. The Research Manager reinforced his points with some figures from his last monthly stamp study. Laurie must have tired of the slanging match as Stephen heard the phones go dead.

From what he heard from the dialogue it could safely be assumed that Dan considered the sort of trip he was preparing for a complete waste.

Although Baxter shared Dan's views on the futility of these exercises, his recent session with the camera had made the whole prospect a rather exciting one and, overriding his earlier apprehensions, he was now actually quite looking forward to it. Dan's cold water treatment and feelings toward such ventures just expressed to Laurie, made him a little indignant. He thought about the Research Managers' own function, the commissioning of awareness studies on a monthly basis to ascertain whether the public's reaction to stamps changed significantly over a four-week period. Short of some appalling publicity or Government decree attitudes would surely remain fairly constant. Stephen therefore came to the conclusion that stripped down to the essentials, Dan's work schedule would be just as superfluous as everyone else's.

This was no time to indulge personal feelings however. Broadly speaking Dan was alright. He talked too much, and couldn't keep a secret, but this was refreshing when there was so much mystery about. Baxter now thought about the second aspect of his mission – creating disruption or chaos at the store opening. No easy task. He mulled over the possibilities dismissing them almost as fast as they occurred to him. Bomb threats of an anonymous nature, cutting off electricity supply, even crashing his car into the store entrance. All of them would undoubtedly achieve their purpose and defer the opening, but with what consequences? The more effective and severe the ploy, the greater the potential for many nights in a police cell, or at best a court appearance. Too tame an approach and the objective would never be met. He would end up like Peter – persona non grata, after just one job. Stephen was in a tough dilemma, he could cope with the spying bit, and possibly make a nuisance of himself in the store, but the other stuff bordered on the criminal, and called for a sapper or sabotage experience for which he was quite untrained.

Dan's marching in unannounced obliterated any further thoughts on the matter. He reiterated everything Stephen had heard through the wall five minutes earlier. Baxter now had his own problems and patient though he was, he did not feel inclined to be a sponge on this occasion. Turpin was known for trapping good listeners for hours on end and was all set for a long session this time when, quite out of the blue, a saviour appeared at the door.

The girl had all the charm of a Russian hotel clerk who had just had her pay docked for a week. 'There will be a meeting in Mr Bugbear's office in half an hour. Everyone is to attend.'

Dan looked up sheepishly, worried that their prior conversation may have been overheard. He became flustered and started shuffling some questionnaires on the table. The proclamation over, the unaccompanied girl serenely conducted herself out and vanished down the corridor.

Dan and Stephen looked at each other puzzled. Another summit meeting? What could it be this time? Neither had the remotest idea.

They were all assembled in RB's suite on the thirteenth floor. It all bore a likeness to the last scene in an Agatha Christie play where all the main suspects in the case are closeted together before the master detective. The line ran as follows: Laurie, DNA, Dan Turpin, Peter Truckley and Baxter. Two other persons were also present – the Sales Manager for Boshko Stores who was looking very grim, and Peter Troston who handled the account for Green Dragon.

The mood was certainly very sullen. Laurie was the last to settle. He kept re-shuffling the chairs nervously as if he wasn't sure whether it was better to be part of the audience or at the boss's side. The rest of the assembly were more sanguine. They merely wanted to know if they would still be on the payroll in an hours time. The stage moved over to RB; 'Gentlemen', he began, 'I want to talk to you today about loyalty.'

Anticipating some sort of showdown, Dan Turpin had used the few minutes beforehand to ensure that his five year presentation tie-pin was in full view of those present. If there was going to be any mudslinging or questioning as to who was a party liner or not, he was not going to come under any scrutiny or suspicion. He was true blue for the Company. Right now that didn't seem relevant as Bugbear swung round and faced Peter Truckley. The boy's face dropped. 'Surely,' he thought to himself, 'this must be the coupe de grace.' He had already begun to send his very short curriculum vitae to several new and untried companies but he realised that surviving just a few months with a one and only employer wasn't exactly the best possible recommendation.

Staring hard at Peter, RB continued. 'Over the last couple of weeks I have found my shoes smothered with wet pink stamps on coming into the building in the morning.'

Now Truckley knew he was a goner. He hung his head low. Someone had seen him floating the stamps out of the window. The game was up. Peter wondered if he could defend his action in any way before sentence was passed. After all, a prisoner condemned to a long sentence notches the walls; he was only killing time in his own manner.

'How long have you been with us, Peter?' Truckley was too numb to reply. He hated being humiliated in front of the others, gathering no comfort from the fact that this was the last time it would happen and that he would probably never see them all again anyway. Better just to run out now.

'Brilliant, quite brilliant' said RB, 'and to think that somebody who's been with us such a short time could devise something as symbolically original as this. So subtle. Treating the opposition as a doormat. What a way to start a day. It just puts you in the right frame of mind to grind them further into pulp. Terrific, Peter, really terrific.'

The bemused Truckley raised his head up again as RB's repeated adjectives started to sink in. Perhaps they had all misjudged the mood of the meeting and more good news was going to follow. Dan Turpin's mind turned to salaries, or more specifically his own. 'Yes' he thought 'that's it'. It was at least six months since his last pay boost – they were all going to be rewarded together. Dan's mind raced ahead. He thought of his own contribution over the last half year. Blank! He couldn't remember anything concrete or outstanding which would merit any kind of a rise. In fact he was hard put to justify what he had done at all. His enthusiasm waned. No he'd jumped the gun. This wasn't a salary review. A false dawn if ever there was one.

'I may as well be frank with all of you' said RB, 'you're not going to like this, but neither do I.'

Those present realised that the time for pats on the back was over. Peter had been the lucky recipient this time, but that was over and done with. They now prepared themselves for the dire tidings due any moment.

'I recently briefed Stephen Baxter for a very important mission. He was to go up to Granline's new Scottish store and do his best to disrupt and sabotage the opening.' No punches needed to be pulled. The assembly were only too aware of the underhand work organized from the thirteenth floor. RB continued. 'We were working on a plan whereby we would have everything ready for his trip up north in a couple of weeks time. And what do I find? Granline opened up yesterday, two weeks ahead of schedule, and the reason why seems pretty obvious. They knew we were going up there so they deliberately pushed things forward a fortnight.' A pause. 'The conclusion, gentlemen, is therefore very plain. We have a Pink spy up here without question. There is no other explanation.'

The shock that something had been done against the Company was a severe one. It was alright for RB and his cronies to get outsiders to apply for positions with Pink and report back, or for Field Sales Managers to deliberately walk into a Pink store and 'persuade' the owner to go Green. It came as a major shock nonetheless to discover that Pinkerton and his team had gone a few steps further in their own 'surveillance and competitor activity' function – they had an insider who was already party to their most clandestine moves. RB resumed his analysis. 'The only person to know about Stephen's trip, apart from myself, would be the person who made his hotel booking. Stephen did you get that far and find a room?'

Before an answer was forthcoming Troston made his presence felt by those around him. He was angry. He had devised, at a high cost to Boshko, a special promotional package to break two weeks hence to counter the Granline inauguration. Considerable effort and many HQ manhours had been expended by Troston and his eighth floor team to fend off the Pink threat, but the leakage just revealed rendered his efforts instantly stillborn.

Baxter felt personally let down, for since his original briefing in this very office he had been all over the place in his effort to prepare himself for the job. It was a funny feeling because during this time he would have given anything to be excused the mission. Like a trip to the dentist, he was keyed up for the visit only to have it called off in this unusual way. For him to suggest the name of anyone in particular who could be thought of as an 'infiltrator' would be absurd. Why, anyone could have to come into his room, picked up his notes, and vanished into the amorphous body of souls that make up the Sugar Cube. He thought of the vulnerability of his office. It was only yesterday that he chatted to the window cleaner whose cradle swung precariously outside his office before lurching upward to spend proportionally longer cleaning the glass on the thirteenth floor. Another suspect then.

RB's first move was to shout for Laurie. His faithful retainer was sitting right in front of him. 'Drop whatever you're doing and start an immediate enquiry. We've got to find this man, gentleman – anymore coups like this one and we could soon find ourselves as the number two trading stamp company.' Laurie stiffened upon hearing his summons. It was the 'whatever you're doing bit' that made him shudder. Divulging his current activity to all and sundry would be a trifle embarrassing. He was conducting an in-house survey to ascertain whether Green Dragon employees considered the ten foot depth of the Country Club swimming pool should be reduced to six foot.

If the guilty party were present at that moment in RB's suite, the knowledge that Laurie was to handle the investigation must have given him much comfort and relief.

Laurie decided to conduct his enquiry in the peaceful surroundings of the Country Club. Not only was he six miles away from head office and no longer at the other end of RB's call button, but he was much happier in this kind of environment. The relaxed atmosphere was an altogether much more palatable proposition as far as he was concerned. He would not have to pretend he was doing something vital. For a change this was actually the case.

The Country Club, bought for tax purposes by the Founder, became the social centrepiece of the Empire in no time at all. Pool, squash courts, drink, everything, all available at rock bottom rates for the staff. As the key figure in this new melodrama, Baxter was summoned by Laurie to give account of his movements in the time lapsed since he was given the original brief. From HQ to the Club took about fifteen minutes as Stephen manouvered his dirty old saloon through the suburbs to his lunchtime date. He now regretted picking up a car he was probably going to be stuck with. He had sorted out a battered old wreck for an abandoned mission and felt highly conspicuous driving round the North London suburbs in a machine which even an impoverished student might disown. Considering the pains taken to select such a banger it seemed rough justice when everyone else in the Company was using one that was new. It didn't seem an appropriate time to ask for it to be changed. Better wait 'till the enquiry was over.

When he got there it was well after three o'clock and there were still a few revellers left in the snooker room located off the main ballroom. The most striking feature was an enormous chandelier hanging down over the dance floor – one that flew out all colours when it was turning. Baxter recognised the boys horsing around with the billiard cues. They were all meant to be back in the transport room, but it was obvious they were now in no condition to get back to head office let alone give out car keys to the sales force.

The place now seemed fairly empty and although there were dozens of small rooms available to him, Laurie had, for some reason, decided to sit himself down in the middle of the ballroom floor on one of the wrought iron chairs which normally belonged outside by the swimming pool. He had evidently dragged it across the floor as a long mark was now etched on the woodblock surface. Baxter caught Laurie's eye and beckoned him over. Stephen grabbed a bar stool and stepped down onto the dance floor and positioned himself a few feet away from his interrogator. The scene was set therefore for trying to unravel the mystery.

Concentration on the business in hand however was severely hindered by a rather absurd sight. A dancing instructor and his girl pupil were tangoing round the room without music. Every twenty seconds or so they would both waft by silently, creating a draft of wind that blew all Laurie's papers off the table. It was naturally a jarring distraction, particularly when the teacher started muttering 'left, glide, forward' with each pass. Initially Laurie was so intent on his job he seemed not to notice until such time as the girl got her footwork wrong and collided with his desk. 'Could they please confine themselves to the other side of the floor, at least until his discussions were over', pleaded Laurie. Stephen steeled himself for further questioning, but unexpected relief was near at hand. The dance inspector, obviously was on a shorter fuse than Laurie had anticipated. He immediately took exception to the request to move out of range, snarling as he made the not unreasonable point that the club was large enough to permit two people to conduct such a meeting in any one of a dozen rooms. Monopolising the one area where he was earning his pin money, was unjustifiably stupid and selfish. Such a challenge to Laurie's authority in the one domain where he still held a little respect and recognition was just too much for him to stand. Several papers from the inquisitor's desk were gently wafting across the highly polished wooden floor. Both men were now squaring up to each other jostling and pushing, whilst the girl seemed as relieved as Stephen that the lesson had come to a premature end. She had looked less and less interested as the gliding around had continued, and had stared longingly at the door which led to the car park. If they were grateful for the respite the two protagonists were offered no such luxury as pride and territory were at stake. Neither fighter could have been said to have been in the best physical condition. The instructor was in all respects a true lightweight scarcely five feet tall and with a pallor typical of someone whose face rarely hit daylight. Laurie's main asset was bulk and in theory it should have stood him in good stead in this predicament. It was the cobra and the mongoose. Laurie was scared stiff but could not afford to show it. Somehow the instructor sensed his opponent's fear and took the initiative in a place where the adversery least expected it – the shin. The dagger sharp stilletto found its mark and Laurie doubled up in pain. Ringside customers would have had a raw deal as the pre-emptive strike brought the bout to an end. Laurie gave ground as flustered and wounded he reckoned suing for peace a less painful process than perhaps having to cope with a couple of punctured ankles. Suitably chastened, he led Baxter up behind the bar where there was a small projection room used mainly by DNA for screening PR films. Laurie renewed the questioning until around five in the afternoon when the slow steady build up of early evening drinkers made noisy inroads to any further interrogation so they packed it in. The overall result was that no evidence was forthcoming which could throw any more light on the matter. Both of them rather hoped the problem would go away and that RB's spy mania would abate when other more significant issues arose. If there was a leak it was not stopped by the enquiry and each person to the original warning upstairs had their own views and suspicions as to the guilty party. The matter would simmer in the background. It could well be that the early opening of Granline was due to internal reasons and had nothing to do with 'agents within'. The onset of filming TV commercials was a welcome interlude and distraction.

4

Maintaining the Empire's image and status in the face of a demanding and fickle public, was the task facing DNA and his brow-beaten publicity team. The budget under his control was balanced in a different way to similar size concerns, owing to the disproportionate amount needed to cover merchandising in all its forms. Since the Company itself was a form of sales promotion, all monies were lumped together and included in the general mix of outgoings without much scrutiny or haggling from the Board.

Douglas thus revelled in a position where he alone, apart from RB, could appropriate funds in whatever direction caught his fancy. He personally chose the advertising agents, photographic studios, distribution houses and film production units who kept the Green god in full view of a stamp orientated public. He was forever being wined and dined by the National Press, each paper vieing with each other to get the lion's share of advertising money. The only area he shunned was the house magazine which he was happy not to be associated with. This was the propaganda sheet shambolically thrown together by Laurie and the Personnel Manager. No kudos here, just masses of inter-department weddings, dart matches, children's fairs, charity appeals, etc. Douglas had reached an advanced stage of planning some TV commercials. The theme behind the campaign would be how the Empire had penetrated everyone's way of life in the nicest possible way, and would focus on several towns with a voice-over describing the impact local gift house and stamp outlets were making on the population regarding jobs and shopping habits. It seemed natural that the initial sixty-second advertisement should concentrate on Green Dragons home base and the executives responsible for bringing so much joy and happiness to a grateful public. It no longer seemed essential to go to the lengths necessary in the early days of the Company's growth where explanations of the modus operandi of the stamp system were deemed mandatory. Since everyone was cognisant of the new order they could now afford to be seen in a corporate light in a similar vein to campaigns for BP or the Wool Council. This assumption did not seem at all presumptious to RB when DNA outlined his plans for the opening film.

'Tell me what you have in mind, Douglas!' said RB, certain that Alcott in his creeping and ingratiating way would somehow glorify RB himself in celluloid. Douglas smiled, gently anticipating RB's thoughts and laid down a storyboard and provisional script before his master. Bugbear studied the drawings and cutouts eagerly. It looked like scenes from a Wagnerian opera – lots of sky, thunder, high places and masses of people. Although mystified at first RB became happier and happier as Douglas explained how this small screen epic would take shape. Haseys, the advertising agency, guided and prodded by DNA had dreamt up the plot.

A hot air balloon was to be placed on the roof of the Sugar Cube. All the hierarchy of Green Dragon were also to be on the roof in smart green blazers. In the foreground the Founder, suitably decked out in parachute gear and flying apparatus, shakes hands with RB, waves goodbye to the Green elite, and takes off into the blue to spread the gospel in uncharted territories beyond.

That, at least, was the theory. Douglas was astute enough to ensure RB a co-starring role which obviously delighted him. He knew whatever the extravaganza finally cost RB would approve it so long as his own part was so visual. The elaborately conceived storyboard, gloatingly admired and praised, gave no indication of the vast production problems involved in this fantasy in the sky. First there was the little matter of getting the balloon atop the Sugar Cube, to say nothing of launching it from such an uncertain base with an actor replacing the Founder for the highly dangerous lift-off. The Sugar Cube was a tower block built in 1959 and was never designed for aerobatics or high jinks on the top deck. There was a cornucopia of air vents, ducts, funnels and rectangular fairings making it a very poor site as a potential launching pad. Several wires and pulleys were also in evidence. From what one knew of the reliability of hot air balloons it seemed that a calm, windless launch from ground level would not necessarily guarantee a perfect lift off, even if managed by a professional ground crew. The combination of the sixteen stone Founder, an unknown actor, and a high unpredictable dirigible had all the ingredients of a nightmare. As the original builders never envisaged any member of the staff ever venturing on to the roof, there was no safety railing round the perimeter, and for this particular exercise, access to the top was only possible via a tiny ladder from a duct on the thirteenth floor! The logistical problems were clearly awesome.

Douglas was confident that men and machines could somehow be assembled according to plan. He therefore concentrated his attention on the dramatic opening shots of the film and getting to grips with what at first seemed to be a major obstacle. The first frames of the storyboard called for a long shot of the Sugar Cube from above, before zooming in on the activity on the roof. Since the tower block was by far the tallest one around, there seemed no way of accomplishing this short of mounting the cameras from a helicopter or aircraft.

There was a solution, but one that would require liquid cash and a fair amount of diplomacy. The suggestion came from RB himself who, having had sight of the script, became totally involved in the venture, temporarily forgetting his preoccupation with spies and traitors. Seeing himself as producer, director and co-star, he had an excellent idea. Four hundred yards away from HQ, across the car park and compound Skipton and Co were constructing a warehouse with the aid of a 300 foot crane. The driver or operator was located almost 250 feet up in a tiny cabin. With a little ingenuity and persuasion, a cameraman could be accommodated therein, thus rendering the loan of equipment-laden aircraft unnecessary. This would be a most difficult phase of production, but if they could just get hold of that crane for half a day it might solve everything.

Getting permission from the contractors would be the stumbling block. Here was an organization quite unaffected by Green Dragon, not short of cash, and with building deadlines to meet. There was, therefore, no reason whatsoever for them to oblige DNA and his crew whatever the inducements. It was obvious then approaches would have to be made to the crane operator without Skipton's knowledge, and the man won over by however much it took. The task was assigned to Peter Truckley. Since Peter possessed neither tact nor diplomacy but did have a kind of open naivety bordering on stupidity, he was as likely to be as successful as anyone else available. To bolster up his chances DNA stuffed his pockets with £5 notes to the tune of £300. That should take care of a days rental at least!

Much to everyone's surprise the operator was most obliging and willing to fall in with the plans. It transpired that he had a personal grudge with his employers, and as a result of his attitude towards them was co-opted on to permanent 'crane detail' and denied the more lucrative bulldozer shift down on ground level. When Peter opted for conducting negotiations in the 'cabin in the sky' the benefits of such a choice became clear to both parties. There would not be witnesses to their transactions. Peter certainly felt he had struck a very good deal both for the Company and himself. He managed to part with just a third of his 'persuasion' allowance, leaving him with a sizeable 'back pocket' profit way beyond anything that had ever come his way before. The operator, for his part, had got himself a day off and £100 into the bargain. The vital aspect as far as DNA and the production team were concerned was that both cameraman and director could both fit comfortably inside the cabin and shoot the opening sequence. Peter came back with a mission completed, a grin, and reported that he had booked the crane two weeks hence with full co-operation all round.

Now this was done, other jobs in the planning of the film were put in hand. The green blazers were an abomination by anyone's standard. There was clearly no time for the garments to be made to measure, and moreover the exact number were procured a day prior to shooting. The jackets were distributed on a first come best choice basis among the Board members. Bright emerald with a rich sage velvet trim on lapels and cuffs, they had a white background on the breast pocket emblazoned with the Green Trading Stamp and a silver border. It reminded one of the obligatory uniform the US President insisted foreign guests wore on their visit to Camp David. The tastelessness was emphasized by the discovery that the two inch staff motif was luminous in the dark. Late night revellers 'phoned the local paper in a panic-stricken state. They had reported seeing ghostly lights waiting across the car park. Three board directors were therefore amazed to be confronted by police cars acting on 'information received' and ready to challenge the white phantoms.

Preparations were as near complete as they were ever going to be. The props were ready and a shooting schedule agreed. It was now up to the 'actors'. Day one of the shoot started early, 6.30 am. Two middle-aged executives stood shivering on the edge of the tarmac airstrip some 20 miles north of London. Richard and Laurie, resplendent in their new gear, waited anxiously for the little yellow executive jet bearing the Founder coming in from his Paris retreat. Within minutes the bird was down and its beaming passenger back in the charge of his two trusted lieutenants. Once all three executives were gracefully purring back to the Sugar Cube in 001 (the Founders black Bristol saloon) the mood prevailing was akin to boy scouts off to camp for the first time. The Founder loved being back 'amongst the boys' again. Despite spending long periods in Paris, Jersey and California, he relished the company of his old cronies, and eagerly looked forward to 'mucking in' in the same way he used to when he was on the road fifteen years earlier. It wasn't quite like the old times though. The years away, following his marriage to a young girl who caught his eye as a model in the first stamp catalogue, had put paid to the relaxed familiarity he once enjoyed with the staff. He was still undoubtedly very popular, but nowadays everyone seemed to treat him with an aura of mystified reverence which in spite of his genial protests, he had been unable to quell.

Laurie, notwithstanding the pitch and roll of the limousine, unfurled the new blazer and assisted his chief into it. With the Founder's enormous bulk this was no easy task. It was an appalling fit. He held his breath and forced the buttons into their respective holes, after which he could barely breathe. It didn't matter. He grinned. There was no way he wasn't going to enjoy himself today. Three glasses materialised out of nowhere, and the early morning took on a rosy glow. Nobody needed that drink more than Laurie. Up at 4 am the responsibility of getting the Founder and RB 'on site' for the cameras rolling at 7.30 am was entirely his. He couldn't believe that everything had gone quite so smoothly up to now. The weather report from across the Channel was fine, so the plane had come down on time. It was still only 7.00 am, both his charges were happy chuckling over old times and, mishaps aside, they would all be on the set with time to spare. He was nonetheless aware that this was only part of the jig-saw. Other people had to come up with the goods too. But, just for the moment, Laurie allowed himself to relax and savour the smooth progression of things. It wasn't very often he was able to do so. If the day closed as well as it had begun it would be a miracle.

Douglas had encountered all sorts of problems in procuring the balloon. It was all very well producing nice storyboards with nice pictures of them; laying his hands on one was a different matter. No-one in his team had given this any thought and it wasn't until three weeks prior to shooting that one was tracked down in an old aircraft hanger at Cardington, Bedford. Out came the cheque book as he took stock for what was becoming a routine move in the acquisition of props. Douglas had insisted upon going to Bedford in person, he suspected that Peter Truckley had concluded a mutually beneficial deal with the crane driver and determined that this time, if there was any 'slush money' around, he would be the sole recipient of any loose change.

Inadequate preparation by his scouts almost killed off the whole show. True enough the balloon and basket were languishing there in a hanger but unbeknown to the Green Dragon entourage the owner had received enquiries from the secretary of the local flying club who wished to hire it as a curtain-raiser to a series of displays over the coming weeks. Douglas and his henchmen drove up to the vast corrugated structure and endeavoured to find the owner. It was like an empty cathedral save for a small partitioned office in the far corner. He marched over and as he did so voices became audible within. The glass partitioning was only four feet high and he could hear every word. His timing was bang on the button. The owner and secretary were coming to terms. Alcott had to act fast. There was no time for pleasantries since the secretary was on the point of signing the form and purloining the balloon. Douglas had survived over the years by opportunism and chance. Once he heard the words 'fee' and 'hire' mentioned he burst into the room. The result was as if two holiday makers were competing for the last paddle canoe at a boating pond. A fist fight did not seem at all unlikely. The balloon owner had already agreed a rate with the secretary when Douglas offered to double it. It immediately became an unfair contest. No club secretary, heavily dependent on raffles, draws, and voluntary subscriptions, could compete with a national giant like Green Dragon represented here by its leading manipulator. The man with the handle-bar moustache stormed at the way he had been 'gazumped' by the vendor. Douglas grinned and laid a 'contract' in front of his overwhelmed partner.

Signatures stamped and delivery date agreed, Alcott and his team triumphantly made their way back to the car. There was little respite for his henchmen as Douglas lambasted his junior colleagues for their slackness in almost having no balloon to haggle over. The air was heavy with his vehemence. It was to get worse in a couple of minutes when one of his underlings wound down the windscreen to eject a cigarette and noticed a flat tyre. All of a sudden there were four flat tyres. The flying club man had been a sore loser. With all the passengers gaping at their sabotaged machine he honked his horn mockingly and roared past them.

The car bearing the Founder, RB and Laurie slithered under the Sugar Cube bang on time. Almost everyone, including the hierarchy, had taken up their positions on the summit where the producer, director, carpenters and their assistants were doing their utmost to organize the set in very cramped conditions. It had all the makings of a rocket launch with the same degree of unpredictability. The basket itself was about six feet square and tethered on all sides by thick ropes. It was decked out in green bunting with overlapping sandbags and was above the gas jet was the huge canvas casing. One side displayed a flattering drawing of the Founder, probably taken from an early photograph when he was a ironmonger. No glasses, paunch, or double chin here, but a filmposter sketch, barely recognisable from the armorphoid now puffing and blowing his way to the top of the building.

There was a considerable amount of danger for actors and artisans alike in the absence of any perimeter fence round the roof. This fear meant they all tended to huddle nervously in the middle, whereas the script called for distance between the balloon and its waving well-wishers. The director sensed this apprehension, making unconvincing proclamations that no-one had ever fallen off as far as he knew, and anyway a complete medical team was standing by for any emergency. Unallayed fears nothwithstanding, the director cajoled his cast to 'take up first positions' for the opening shot. It was here that the Founder had to clamber into the wicker container and be filmed smiling and waving, after which he would be replaced by a special stunt actor for the actual lift off. Those assembled who took particular note of the boss when he first came up would have seen how pale he looked. Warnings about 'falling off' and 'medical teams' had done nothing to bolster his confidence. The adrenalin of the big occasion, topped up by the reinforcements on the drive from the airstrip, had rapidly drained away. With some folk it's spiders, others snakes, but as far as the boss was concerned it was exposed heights. He looked progressively more and more nervous and was clearly terrified that once in the basket, the contraption would break its guy lines, and roar off into the blue with him inside.

As the camera whirled, the assistant director called for a uniform grin. The shot lasted five seconds. One take. No problems. Shot two would show the Founder in the basket. The director ordered the cameraman to swivel round for a similar burst on the boss. The focus puller and lighting cameraman made their adjustments. Sudden panic. Where was the Founder? Everyone's eyes were fixed on the empty balloon basket. Laurie rushed forward and managed to rip his jacket on one of the arc-light stanchions in his eagerness to find the boss.

About twenty pairs of eyes leaned over the rim of the basket. The Founder was crumpled up on the rush-mat floor. He had either fainted outright or had had a heart attack whilst everyone was concentrating on the opening sequence. This was very serious indeed. Carlo Mucatta, the Italian director, lent over the side jabbering furiously and cursing this fresh turn of events. He had rightly anticipated the difficulties regarding the acquisition of props but looked forward to a trouble free run with his 'artists'. He thought back to how he was persuaded to take on this commercial in the first place, having publicly declared that TV ads were demeaning to his reputation and unworthy of his talent. Now this. It was true that many actors had walked off his set and that others had thrown tomatoes at him after heavily charged scenes, but never, never, had anyone, let alone his key figure and patron, died on him before.

With the aid of walkie-talkies relayed to the ground, help was not long in coming. The noise of the balloons gas jet which had been roaring away for some time, was now drowned by the whine of helicopter blades as the Red Cross chopper picked out the last few square feet of vacant roof space. Three men in white coats jumped out and bundled the bulbous figure of the Founder onto a stretcher and up into the helicopter.

RB grabbed Mucatta's megaphone from a dithering Laurie Rabbler, telling everyone to remain calm and that despite the tragedy the show would go on. He then pulled together Mucatta and Alcott for a parley. They agreed upon a compromise situation to save the film. Instead of concentrating on the Founder's face, the camera would be positioned behind the balloon to show a man waving to the directors. The pan would be too short for all but the Founders closest confederates to make out that someone other than the boss was aboard.

By the time Mucatta and his entourage had got themselves ready for this new shot, another factor had come into the reckoning – the weather. It was drizzling barely noticeably when the 'cast' initially took up their positions. The Founder's demise and rapid exit had so held everyone's attention that the rain was of little consequence. Now that there was a lull, people were aware of the elements. The heavy downpour was joined by a strong wind which at some 200 feet above ground took on tornado proportions.

Another dilemma and a further huddle between the big 'three'. Yes, they would press on. Although a casual observer would judge this as pure madness, current circumstances demanded it, since both booking the balloon and stunt actor for a further session were out of the question. The Founder's 'fill in' was already signed up for a parachute jump into the open sea extolling the virtues of a waterproof watch.

The actor clambered in and felt a gentle crunch under his feet. The Founder's glasses. The rain lashed his face as he nervously donned the crash helmet and goggles. The situation was urgent. Getting the balloon off and away and the sodden cast off the roof was A1 priority. Just standing upright was now a challenge as Mucatta snapped his fingers, the camera rolled, and the ropes released. There could be no second takes here. All responsibility rested with the camera operator as the huge device blasted upward. The sheer speed of the vertical ascent took the whole crew by surprise so that the operator had no angle to play with and the storyboard became a complete irrelevance. The original plan, drawn up so that the balloon would make an angle glide thus keeping the name and logo in view, went completely by the board. So low was the cloud base it vanished into the murky sky with disarming haste. The actor went on waving frantically as long as those below could still see him. The gesture was useless since he may as well have been enveloped into a black hole hanging directly over the Sugar Cube.

Further alarming thoughts crossed the director's mind. Could the 'stand in' successfully bring his chariot back to earth? Were those disappearing waves desperate appeals for help? Could he make ignominious history by becoming the first director responsible for two fatal mishaps in the making of one sequence? As he pondered these unpleasantries the rest of the crew quickly abandoned their positions, eager to resuscitate themselves via a buffet lunch which Laurie had laid on at the Red Feathers across the street.

It was comforting to relate that neither the Founder nor the unlucky actor met his maker that day. The Boss had suffered an acute attack of agoraphobia and had merely fainted from shock. The unfortunate actor had been genuinely petrified and revealed afterwards that when he suddenly became enveloped in gloom, he thought his number was up. He had kept his head however, and nerve ends very stretched, and had ended up in a field some fifteen miles away.

The film was shown as a sixty second commercial in the early summer after considerable changes to the original script. Vivienne's research girls reported a heavy awareness of the campaign which was reflected in business terms when Akos restaurants, a chain of Greek eating houses, started giving stamp vouchers with meals a move triggered off by the owner's son watching the commercial.

RB was full of enthusiasm for a second dip into film making, and asked Laurie (of all people!) to come up with ideas to top the balloon theme. This he duly did and, mindful of the Managing Director's liking for an all-action approach plus some personal involvement, opted for an outrageously ridiculous plan. The venue this time would be Southampton Water and co-operation with the Navy an essential ingredient. Laurie envisaged a quiet stretch of water suddenly disrupted by an emerging submarine. Once on the surface, the hatch on the conning tower opens and up comes the Founder in naval uniform. Whilst a flag is raised in company colours, small rowing boats approach the vessel full of clamouring housewives waving saver books.

Laurie was invited to C in C Fleet Portsmouth to submit his proposals and report back on their reaction. Despite the Navy's willingness to help, the plans never left RBs desk. The fact that it was considered in the first place was rather amazing. To start off with, it was highly unlikely that the Founder, following his near demise in the balloon, would gladly allow himself to be incarcerated in the boat's hull and make an exit in full camera view. Even this took for granted his ability to clamber through the hatch. Stand-ins could again be used, though as an addition to an already unrealistic budget, burdened with bit-part fees for the housewife extras.

The other point about the exercise was that although the theme of the Company's ubiquitousness was emphasised (even under water!) it was more or less the same story as before, the difference this time being the enormous location costs, coupled with paying off a complement of sailors for their technical assistance.

5

Christmas was approaching and with it the function most eagerly anticipated by the 5,000 card holders of the Empire: the annual free-for-all at the Royal Lancaster Hotel in the West End of London. Stephen, for one, felt the need for some kind of celebration; after all, he had been with the Company almost a year now and witnessed all kind of behaviour from every quarter, and yet had himself played the game according to the rules. It seemed to him that pre-occupation with opposing stamp schemes, losing accounts, or government decrees hostile to trading stamps were dying down. The holiday mood and festive parties were upon them. Personal vendettas, politics and the like could be put to one side for a while. There was a general slackening of inhibitions in every department that made up the Sugar Cube.

Peter Truckley used the lax mood prevailing as an opportunity to torment the young ladies of hotel administration. He would phone down giving them a list of towns he was visiting and make absurd accommodation requests he knew were impossible to satisfy. The whole section would be plunged into turmoil as he demanded a YMCA room in Norwich, a five star in Derby, and a moslem meal only in Kings Lynn. The poor girl unfortunate enough to pick up the phone would labour innocently on these non-starters before Peter would get onto the supervisor and say the whole thing was an administrative error and to forget it.

No-one revelled in the holiday mood more than Vivienne Darcy-Flong, Dan Turpin's assistant, who directed all the outside girls. She had a flat just about a mile away from head office and most of the hierarchy dropped in on her from time to time, in and out of business hours. She had all her data in the apartment, plus a liberal amount of liquid bonhomie for her callers. The day before the main party at the Lancaster Hotel, Vivienne threw her own party for the Marketing

Department as a curtain-raiser, and included RB and Laurie for good measure. Even these people seemed that much more pleasant outside the suffocating atmosphere of the Sugar Cube. Privilege and status die hard however, and RB still expected Laurie to fill his glass and drip feed him with nuts. In the meantime, in the absence of tolerable female company, Stephen Baxter joined Peter in Vivienne's kitchen. An unguarded bottle of port was standing in the corner. Mellowing fast and increasingly oblivious to others present, both of them got into the mood for a joke affecting a third party. The bottle was two-thirds gone when Peter laid his cards on the table. He took off his gold tie pin and matching Waterman pen, and gazed at Baxter who gaped back uncomprehendingly. Peter was prepared to stake both items against whatever his friend happened to have in his wallet that he would be the one to spend that night in Vivienne's flat. Baxter checked out the state of the wallet. He found a few calling cards and £15 worth of special purchase vouchers which he proposed cashing in on his next trip to the gift house. The bargain struck, both of them lurched out of the kitchen to face those remaining in the lounge. Virtually everyone had gone, bar a couple of Vivienne's interview girls who had now crashed out on the sofa. The hostess's work files and books were scattered all over the room – it was a terrible mess; the only consolation being that there were no other potential contenders left accidentally to mess up their wager. Baxter had drunk marginally less port than Peter and was still able to focus properly. He concentrated what energy he had left in consolidating his game plan. To do this meant joining Vivienne on the floor as she struggled to collect various pieces of paper strewn all over the carpet. Still holding a gin and tonic in one hand she mumbled something about losing important documents, but Baxter's attentiveness distracted her from her purpose, and after half an hour's blurry conversation they slowly meandered towards Vivienne's bedroom. Stephen's eyes lit up as things were going his way. A dull thud eminated from the other side of the room. Peter had passed out. 'Set, match, pen and tiepin' thought Stephen. 'What a way to win.'

Baxter woke up the following morning with a raging thirst and a thumping head. He felt awful. He realised he was alone in the bed. The aroma of last night's drink and cigar smoke was trapped in the flat, and he made his way into the lounge with difficulty. He wondered where on earth his clothes were and, for that matter, where Vivienne had gone. A note on the coffee table gave him the answer. It told him that she had let him go on sleeping and also reminded him that the presentation of the annual Five Year loyalty awards by the Founder of the Empire was to be made at 9.30 at the Country Club. Every Christmas he would fly in from Jersey in his green Lear jet, then shoot back again before the taxman could realise what was afoot.

Picking up his ill-gotten tie pin, he tried to put in into his bare chest. A stabbing pain reminded him he was wearing neither shirt nor tie and locating one or the other might be advantageous as a first step to attending this function. Certain people might have noted his behaviour last night and failing to put in an appearance this morning would be a mistake. It was now five to nine and the immediate priority was finding his clothes, an aspirin for his head, and getting to the Country Club for the 9.30 start. All he had been wearing the previous night was in a heap by the bed with the exception of one sock; the absence of which in a few minutes would become an urgent problem. He ran upstairs to the bathroom, swallowed two white tablets indiscriminately and prepared to leave minus the one sock. He consoled himself during the quick drive to the Club that several of last night's gang would be sitting down at the ceremony in an equally devastated state.

He made it bang on the button. Thank God, he thought, he didn't have to get up and receive anything himself. He found a seat at the back of the hall and feigned a little interest at the Founder's opening words. The speech was punctuated by sporadic applause which caused Stephen a lot of pain. He tried to keep his head down almost on his knees, and felt very sick indeed. It was in this comotose state that Stephen was half aware of a hand reaching out from the chair behind him with a note scribbled on a piece of paper. Even in his condition he recognised the scrawl. The shadowy script of DNA.

The last thing Stephen wanted to do was to concentrate on anything. He promptly offered the note back from whence it came, hoping it was just a polite instruction to everyone to leave quietly at the end or join in the cheers for the Founder at the appropriate time. This cosy notion soon evaporated as the note was again pressed into his hand, only now his name was written on the top. He read it. The contents made him dribble into his handkerchief. If ever there was a low watermark in Baxter's life this was surely it. It transpired that

Alcott's assistant, Roger Shrapnell, was due to be presented with his gold pin but a driving accident meant he wasn't around to receive it; and as DNA was himself in the projection room preparing a film for Boshko executives who were also at the ceremony, could Stephen possibly accept the award in his place? Baxter was mortified. If he could just find Truckley to do this one thing he would gladly return all last night's gains. Peter, needless to say, was nowhere to be seen. He was almost certainly dead to the world somewhere in Vivienne's flat. Baxter studied the order of play as well as his eyes would allow. Judging the speed and progress of the Founder's disposal of honours so far, Stephen reckoned on having about ten minute's grace before his elevation to the presentation platform. At this juncture one further nightmare occurred to him. The dais or platform upon which the dispensations were being allotted was a good four feet above the audience in the auditorium. There was no way in which he could walk up there and stop everyone noticing the fact that he had only one sock on. Desperate times called for desperate measures, there was no time for pleasantries, he had to borrow a sock and fast.

Among those invited to the proceedings were several of Green Dragons major customers including a large delegation from Boshko, plus one or two proprietors of the voluntary chains often run by Asians, and nearly always susceptible to the Green Dragon plan. One such gentleman was sitting to Baxter's right and in an instant this person found himself the subject of a rather strange request. Amazingly enough and much to Stephen's relief, his neighbour obliged without the slightest qualm. The fact that one of his socks was royal blue and the other magenta did not matter. If he let his trousers down a bit they should cover the instep and all would be well. In no time at all Shrapnell's name echoed around the hall. Stephen got up and did his stuff, taking care not to trip over the sagging trousers. He received the gold pin and felt as if a great weight had been taken off him. His head was clearing now and the ceremony was coming to an end. The Founder, sensing how well things had gone so far, and in an aura of good will had decided to extend the affair briefly by personally thanking all Green Dragon clients who had supported the meeting. Sir Stamford Brook himself, in a comfortable chair, stepped up to receive a tankard from the Founder. It was at this point that something went awfully wrong. As a final gesture and also to prove to the assembly that Boshko was not the only customer to be given the red carpet treatment, the Founder wished to shake the hand of Asif Igpal, owner of the chain of small grocery emporiums clustered around the London area. This, needless to say, was the man who had just surrendered his sock to Stephen. Asif went up and received another tankard amid amused whispers. His particularly short, ill-fitting suit with trousers clearing the ground by several inches made his bare ankle embarrassingly visible.

The Christmas Party itself differed only in scale from the hundreds of others taking place in London on that particular evening. Dozens of coaches would descend on the Lancaster Hotel and disgorge their suburban cargo at 6.30. By 7.15 many of the Empire's most junior subjects were finding the onslaught of sweet champagne and French wine just a bit too much. By 8 o'clock the foyer resembled a small battle ground and many of the hotel staff, no doubt tipped off by more experienced colleagues, were nowhere to be found. The arrival of the Founder, RB and the other directors was the sign for the waiters to reappear. Such was the lavishness displayed at this point in the Company's fortune that no expense was spared in providing a super cabaret for the occasion – in this case the band of the Grenadier Guards. The resplendent soldiers arrived at about 11 o'clock and many of them must have had the impression they were back on active duty rather than colourful entertainers putting on a show. Had they come a couple of hours earlier there might have been a larger and more attentive audience plus a clean floor upon which to march up and down. Trundling over the debris of glasses, bodies and green vegetation in the form of spilt salad, the guards gave a good account of themselves.

Before long the coaches were reappearing to collect the remnants of persons still able to clamber aboard. Party time was over for another year.

The Company continued to grow. Turnover had reached over fifty-five million and although this was a tremendous achievement the Indian Civil Service would now seem a lean labour-effective concern by comparison. The main recipient for these refugees from the suburbs were the huge amorphous departments of ancillary services which filled up most of the vacant space in the Sugar Cube. Another building two miles away was acquired to take up the overspill. The tenants of the twelfth floor, safe in the knowledge that they themselves were not required to sell stamps, slowly and gradually became isolated from the day-to-day rigours of maintaining the Empire. Having seen the other occupants of the Cube via such occasions as the Christmas party, they tried to keep themselves as far apart as possible.

Pretty soon the rest of the Company became almost totally ignorant of the functions of those persons one floor below the directors. It was into the esoteric atmosphere of the twelfth floor that Falina Varna found herself swept into the department. A black-eyed gypsy from Sibelink in Yugoslavia, she had long greasy jet black hair and eyes to match. She wore a peasant carpet dress on the day she arrived, which soon became quite a talking point among her new fraternity. The amused comments became less complimentary however, when it became apparent that Falina possessed nothing else but her carpet garb and cossack boots. In no time at all the invitations to attend meetings where her presence was required became less frequent, due to the increasing pungence of hair, dress and very strong body odour. One further characteristic endeared her even less to her new colleagues. Without warning, and in no relation to the mood she was in at the time, she would gather saliva and suddenly hurl a ball of spit across the room. The effect of Falina's appearance was to deter many of the tea ladies from making their daily trip upstairs to the top of the building. Rumours of a strange witch wafted below. Meanwhile there was one more addition to the family – Eugene O'Hara also came upstairs after a short spell of working in Public Relations below.

The scene was now complete and the staff complement full. It was at some cost to Stephen's privacy. His office was extended to make one vast room which was then divided into three sections for himself, Falina and Eugene. The Croatian demanded the centre cubicle and neither Stephen nor Eugene felt it an issue worth disputing. The Irishman and Baxter found an immediate rapport, an alliance worth cultivating considering the presence of the hissing primadonna now sitting herself down in the middle. All three were given entirely different briefs. Stephen was now, to all intents and purposes, RB's personal spy in reconnaissance missions to report back to the Managing Director on everything that caught his worried attention. Eugene was to be engaged on a single project – an in-depth analysis of discount stores. Laurie asked Eugene how long he would need to finish this job. The easy going Irishman who was quite capable of taking half an hour to peel an orange, opted for up to a year to complete his research. Most of his information could be gleaned from grocery magazines entailing the minimum of effort – a prospect that suited Eugene just fine. Falina proclaimed herself a think-tank and undertook to investigate the validity of the whole stamp movement.

All three of them found a sort of independence they had not known before, for although they were still part of this large family, their comings and goings were never really called into question. Insofar as it was possible with its mixed inmates and the bizarre nature of some of their duties, a working pattern was established and a kind of routine acknowledged. It suited Eugene and Falina for separate reasons. The former, since he could follow a schedule which allowed him a good opportunity for a cat-nap in the afternoons, and the latter because she could walk in and out as she pleased, snarl, hiss and be as objectionable as the mood would take her.

Stephen became the least satisfied with the arrangement. The others could plod on unmolested, whereas Stephen was fast replacing Laurie as RB's pet ferret and investigator. Now for the first time since joining up he felt at odds with the Company. The mystique and wonderment of the early days had long since passed. Now he needed a worthwhile challenge, preferably unclouded by undercover work. He was becoming a little cynical and although the Empire seemed to fill a void in other people's lives, it certainly was not filling his own. Stephen's frequently meandering thoughts were interrupted by yet another call from above. This time there was a definite change for the better. It was more than that and it promised all he had been hoping for.

Rather than being sent outside investigating rival stores, he was at last to be given a very important position looking after the number one client – Boshko Stores. It would not be concerned with liason and keeping them happy, but more a kind of security officer in charge of all the top secrets pertaining jointly to Boshko and Green. The Granline leak, if that's what it was, must never be allowed to recur, and so with this in Bugbear's mind he decided that a special secret room was to be fitted out just along the corridor from Stephen's own office, and would include every known fact relating to their number one breadwinner and all their rival operators. It would be the Company safe – inpenetrable to outsiders!

The programme of fitting out the 'ops' room seemed akin to

installing a new bathroom in the Kremlin. Enormous attention to detail, absurd diversion of men's time to the task, curiosity from the masses who seemed to know everything about it despite it being a hush-hush project. This traffic of men, boxes, signs and display units to the twelfth floor was a give-away to even the least aware that something was afoot. The end result was a complete anti-climax – a fifteen foot square windowless cell devoted to Boshko; turnover figures, proposed sites, share of the market, names of managers all charted and pinned to the walls. The noise extractor fan gave the impression of being in the ward room of a submarine and anybody obliged to loiter there for more than half-an-hour was guaranteed a thumping headache. When the carpenters firmly packed their bags for the last time it marked more than just the end of all the disruption that had gone on for weeks. It was a watershed pre-empted by one side in the struggle with another. The phoney war between Pink and Green was over as far as RB was concerned. The shock of a planted infiltrator had forced him to build this infernal fortress – a defensive shelter impervious to would-be saboteurs, be they outsiders or inside moles.

One morning Stephen found a heavily padded envelope on his desk. Discarding the wrapping, a heavy brass key dropped out plus a set of instructions. They were in RB's hand. Stephen was to be in sole charge of the room and the security of the material his sole responsibility. At no time was anyone allowed inside without written authorisation from either of them. This was not the only precaution. Either end of the passage flanking the op's room would have an infra-red camera system which would activate a red light both ends when someone passed by.

The fitting out period allowed Baxter a little time to himself away from the office. With fishing rod and a pile of books he took up Eugene's offer of his Waterford cottage for two week's fresh air. The return to the harsher world was a jarring shock. Before long copious notes would arrive on Stephen's desk marked confidential; much from the Green Dragon sales team in the form of field reports and so on, and also every new item relating to Boshko, including several thoughts and views of Sir Stamford himself.

Stephen suddenly felt a little more important than at any stage since joining. The fact that he was now in control of this secret store of information meant that most of the senior personnel from within the

Sugar Cube plus the omnipotent client, were obliged to speak to him for anything they wanted. Less agreeable, and a good deal more blatant, was the increasing amount of communication he was now receiving from DNA. During the first week of Stephen's stewardship Alcott phoned him suggesting a lunch between them. He took the opportunity to remind Stephen of the close links that must be established between his publicity machine and this new information bureau. All the time Alcott assumed he would have access to the room whenever he wanted, and never contemplated any restrictions to one like himself. Douglas even suggested they drive out to a restaurant in St Albans, a long way from head office, where they could talk frankly on their 'new relationship'. Stephen realised that Douglas had never bothered to take much notice of him before and that clandestine lunches in the country were a brazen attempt to ensure he had one foot permanently in the 'ops' room.

In other directions the scene from Stephen's point of view had unexpectedly taken a turn for the better. His perpetual sorties round the country seemed to have come to a temporary halt for which he was most grateful. Neither Falina nor Eugene, in spite of their closeness, seemed at all perturbed by his new role or the stream of eminent visitors who started to pay him visits.

One of the first persons to arrive since the inception of the client command centre was Roger de Lorean of Boshko.

His rise within the retailing store was phenomenal. Originally he joined Boshko as a simple check-out boy before rising to supermarket manager, and was soon offered the position of Marketing Manager of the Group, following the colossal success of each store under his management.

It was natural, therefore, that if anyone should rightly be the first person to inspect the new room it would be himself. He was tough, rude, arrogant and well suited to be Sir Stamford's battering ram in the uncompromising world of food retailing. Unlike others at Boshko he was not convinced of the effectiveness of stamps, so here was the chance to study the way things were organized.

His arrival coincided with one of those afternoons when the department was at its most inactive. Such was the laxness that there were strong similarities to a Mediterranean beach resort rather than a pulsating business empire. This mood prevailed despite Dan Turpin's foresight to send a memo round to everyone on the floor warning all and sundry of the de Lorean visit. It fell on waste ground. This was because there was such a plethora of unnecessary directives floating around on just about every topic under the sun that scant attention was paid to one more particular edict. The ordinary circulars were in plain thin envelopes. Anything from the thirteenth floor came in a highly distinctive cream one guaranteeing it being read since it might concern salary, conditions, prizes or bonuses. Dan's warning came plain and thin and was thus summarily ignored.

Given the wrong instructions by an inexperienced receptionist, de Lorean found himself wandering around the map room before being correctly dispatched to the twelfth floor. He had been advised to turn right when coming out of the lift, walk round the corridor and take the third door along the passage. De Lorean's thinking was such that if once given bad advice you have to assume every other person in the place was equally unreliable. He therefore ignored the third door bit and opened the first open door he could find. It belonged to Eugene O'Hara. The Irishman was slumped low in his chair having dropped from an upright position to the point where his head was practically level with the desk top. He was fast asleep. A copy of the *Irish Times* lay open at the racing page and the floor was conspicuous for several slips of paper of equal size scattered over the carpet. One of them was anchored down by a heavy paperweight. The name of the horse matched that in bold type on the newspaper and was probably Eugene's only winner of the afternoon.

Hugely relieved that this was not Baxter, de Lorean pressed on to suddenly find himself in Falina's presence. A blazing row was in progress, between her and a boy friend on the other end of the line. De Lorean thought long and hard. Was he in the Green Dragon building or in a fish market on the Adriatic? The client remained unnoticed while the argument grew hotter. Serbo-Croatian expletives flowed liberally, the term 'magaracs' occurred three times a sentence. The client was certainly getting an education. So strong did the dispute seem that he reckoned on slipping out before she realised anyone was around. She provided him with his cue. She took the phone away from her mouth, spat generously into it and slammed it down. Shaking both arms into the air, she flew over towards the open window stuck her head outside and screamed into the mid-afternoon air.

De Lorean was convinced he was in the wrong establishment. He sidled out into the corridor. Yes, there were pictures of the Founder there and stamp motifs on the walls. He wasn't crazy though he couldn't speak for others he'd seen. Before he could come to his senses he was directly accosted by Vivienne in a high state of excitement.

'At last,' she moaned, 'so you've come to fix the heating. You're the third man we've had up this morning. It's so hot we're all suffocating here.' Mistaken for the engineer, de Lorean blew up. He'd had enough. He shouted his name, company and purpose to Vivienne quivering with frustration. She apologised, unsure whether to smile at her mistake or just find Stephen as soon as possible. De Lorean had brought with him several rolled up charts, all of which had now become screwed up and unworthy of presentation. He was a man of few words – a lifelong slog battling it out in the abrasive world of retailing had shortened his already limited vocabulary to 'how much', 'will it sell' and 'make me an offer'.

'I expect you want to see the room,' said Stephen following a rejected handshake from his alienated client. The look said it all. He had been in the building for what seemed like hours without fulfilling any objective whatsoever. Both of them marched off to the Op's room. Now where was the key? A panicky thought crossed Stephen's mind – he had lent it to Dan Turpin who wanted to store a set of china he had bought his wife in the Company sale.

The last thing the client wanted to do was to be forced into another introduction. Turpin was the sort of man who stretched the most trivial anecdote into a half-hour sermon, and here he was in contact with the rudest and most abrupt man in retailing. Stephen, painfully aware of the characteristics of both men, and highly conscious of the bad start de Lorean had made, could do nothing as Dan settled into a long rambling treatise on his family holiday in the Channel Islands. He was about to produce some snaps from his wallet when de Lorean interjected.

'Mind if we get on,' he snapped.

Suddenly all three were rudely shaken by a tremendous crash in the passage. A wheel had come off one of the tea ladies' trolley, and the giant tea urn was rolling steadily down the corridor, disgorging its dark brown fluid between the lifts and the adjacent offices. Stephen pretended to ignore it and, key in hand, led de Lorean through the saturated passage to their destination. At least they were both free of Dan, thought Stephen. If they didn't run into anybody else there was still a chance of salvaging something from such an unfortunate visit.

Any such hopes lasted less than ten seconds. As he turned the key in the Op's room door he remembered that the electricians had installed some new wall lighting the previous day but had removed the bulbs, promising to return with specially tinted ones. They had not come back. It would be pitch black in there! Stephen fumbled with the lock conscious of de Lorean at his back as he feverishly sought an excuse to offer the man from Boshko.

Fortunately the overall lighting within the Sugar Cube was particularly bright. Stephen reckoned that if he positioned his guest just inside the open door then hopefully sufficient light would find its way inside. It was a bizarre notion but he felt that any more mishaps would induce de Lorean to abort his mission – the whole account could change to Pink Stamps and he would be out on the streets. Miraculously, de Lorean seemed not to notice the absence of light in the room and got down to business immediately. Unfurling the crumpled charts he produced the latest turnover returns from Boshko's flagship stores, plus some turnover estimates for competitive outlets in the same areas giving Pink.

'Pin these on the wall – that is if you can see the wall!' Stephen acknowledged the need for another excuse and prepared to offer an explanation. De Lorean didn't allow him the chance.

'These figures are red hot. Are you sure no-one can get in here?' Stephen shook his head.

'By the way, I'm all for subdued lighting but not this subdued, damn it! I can't see a thing!'

As Stephen grabbed the material from him he realised he was going to have a problem himself finding some blank wall. It was like the blindfolded man pinning the tail on a donkey.

De Lorean, meanwhile, was having trouble with his seat. In the half gloom which prevailed this was not especially surprising. He shuffled about continuously struggling to get comfortable.

The only good point to emerge so far was that the client had somehow interpreted the lack of light and general discomfort as a deliberate security safeguard built into the general planning.

The time passed very slowly and barely twenty minutes later de Lorean, still fidgeting unceremoniously, made to stand up so as to bring the audience to a welcome end. He did so with a dull crack. For the entirety, he had been perched on Dan's box of china.

Stephen now determined to get his visitor out of the Sugar Cube as quickly as he could. De Lorean emerged from the room blinking bemusedly with an as yet undiscovered tear in his trousers from the staples of the china box. Stephen rightly assumed that de Lorean was convinced that the marketing strategy of his company was being run by a bunch of half-wits and lunatics. It was also a fair comment that no mishap could inflict any further damage on him or his colleagues than already was the case. He winced when he visualised de Lorean telling the Boshko board the nightmare he'd been through. It didn't bear thinking about!

The end of the road was not yet quite in sight, however. As the two men came down the corridor they were obliged to pick their way through the mass of sodden tea leaves, the presence of which had now permeated the entire floor. The client swore loudly each time fresh brown spots splattered over his ankles. As they approached the lifts a deep moaning noise could be heard behind the elevator shaft. It was Laurie. He had obviously belted round the ninety-degree turn completely unaware of the tea spillage and had duly paid the price. He was now crumpled up on the linoleum, reeking of Orange Label blend, his new light grey suit transformed into a tacky sepia one. Stephen felt obliged to rush forward and aid his fallen comrade. De Lorean stood still. There was no way he was going to risk being dragged down into the mire for the sake of another incompetent clown. Besides, he felt a complete wreck anyway. Laurie struggled to his feet and offered de Lorean his hand. This was one more experience the latter could well have done without. Dishevelled and creased after his unhappy session with Baxter he offered his own hand with the enthusiasm of an untouchable greeting a leper. Laurie, passing off his own state as if it were a daily occurrence, smiled tamely and asked Roger if he had had a good day at HQ and was happy with the way things had gone so far. A four-year old child could have gauged de Lorean's demeanour just on the strength of the last few minutes, but Laurie was someone who would not have recognised that a lion was angry until such time as his head was in its mouth. Roger made his last stand. He stared hard at both of them, shook his head violently, and ran down the stairs as fast as he could. Whilst Laurie looked on aghast Stephen tacitly accepted an end like this was inevitable after the sort of day now coming to a close.

The sound of de Lorean's furious footsteps became ever fainter as he spiralled frantically from the twelfth all the way down to the bottom. Stephen gave Laurie no explanation. He strolled into his own office and stood by the window waiting for de Lorean to emerge below and jump into his car. He even thought of waving – that really would rub salt into the wound! Stephen watched the bedraggled figure scurry over the tarmac towards an ostentatious honey-coloured saloon, sandwiched between two well worn HQ Escorts. So tightly did Roger appear to be hemmed in that even from his perch in the sky Stephen could see he was going to have trouble merely getting into the driving seat. He eventually did so, but not before several contortions and twists. Once in, he backed out with a reckless lunge. From his vantage point, and with the late afternoon sun highlighting the subject of his attention, Stephen caught a broadside view of the car as it flashed out of the park. His aerial had somehow sheared off and there was a five foot gash along the side of the saloon.

Baxter moved away from the window. The hum of the company sign again told him close of play was at hand. The masses had started their evening migration and were radiating in all directions to their homes in the suburbs. With snow on the ground and factory chimneys as a backcloth, it could have been a scene from a Lowry painting.

Stephen wondered what the implications and repercussions of the afternoon's proceedings would be.

6

The scene has changed, to the country headquarters of the nation's number one food retailer – Boshko Stores Ltd. A large imposing mansion which Sir Stamford eagerly acquired when the local squire failed to produce enough revenue to prevent it from falling into decay. Surrounded by imposing trees and gardens, a high security fence, and with a long winding drive up to the main entrance, it is a palatial establishment whose new occupants share little in common with the previous owners.

It is a Sunday afternoon and there are loud voices wafting out of what used to be the library. Stag heads, family crests and ornamental carvings oversee the proceedings in this, Sir Stamford's 'state' room, where he meets top executives on weekends if there is something vital to discuss. The last time such a meeting was convened was when Sir Stamford decided to canonise himself as Life President of Boshko. His bronze bust, commemorating his elevation to this estate is sitting in the main hall and impossible to miss. Each Boshko employee, from the humblest check-out girl upward, is encouraged to make a pilgrimage here as part of their induction programme. Sir Stamford himself grew tired of the sculpture and would have been content to see it less prominently placed – a move successfully countered by his wife.

The Board was debating the whole question of trading stamps. Roger de Lorean was there was well needless to say, vociferously opposed to maintaining the system. He is not yet a Board member, and whilst able to exert great influence on the others, is unable to carry enough weight alone to swing the vote against the motion. Several bottles of water, beer and whisky are placed round the room. It has all the makings of a long session. Two heavy individuals, warehouse packers during the week, are told to sit outside and let no-one near those inside.

The timing of this summit could not have occurred at a worse time for de Lorean. Twice divorced, his current girl-friend was already wondering whether Boshko was his entire life and was on the brink of leaving him. His mother had died on Wednesday but he had eschewed a family gathering this afternoon for this current top-level undertaking. If things became really heavy it was doubtful whether he could attend the funeral tomorrow.

The agenda was not merely to decide whether to switch from Green to Pink or even Blue, it was tied in with results just made public in all the trade papers. These showed Boshko slipping badly from their pre-eminent position in sales and profits. These unwelcome figures coincided with the very poor image that Boshko had acquired in the early days, as a cheap and cheerful emporium, and had been further denigrated by the gawdy obtrusive stamp displays in all their outlets. Up to the present time the Boshko/Green combination had ensured them top supermarket slot at the expense of ever being seen as a high quality establishment. The cost of maintaining stamps added at least 15 per cent on top of normal costs despite massive discounts not enjoyed by the smaller Green customers. The issues at stake before the meeting were finely balanced. If current trends were sustained Boshko would continue to lose ground yet still fork out mammoth merchandising costs. They could either promote Green even more heavily by offering ten times the number of stamps against their current treble/quadruple rate, so blitzing Granline and forcing them to offer equal quantities of Pink, or they could take the unthinkable step of dropping stamps altogether. Any poker player faced the same dilemma – either raise the stakes or get out of the game for good!

From the other side of the valley, the imposing Georgian mansion could be seen only in outline as evening closed in on the idyllic country setting. Half past eight and the church bells in the village had long since ceased. The raucous laughter from within the pub cut deeply into the night air. Up on the hill in the Boshko sitting room other voices were also in evidence, but with no hint of laughter and precious little goodwill around.

Eleven o'clock and the chandeliered lights were still bearing witness to the struggle going on in this eighteenth century edifice. Round about midnight all the protagonists in this internal, and what also seemed eternal, battle got up from their seats and made their own individual moves. A decision had been reached. Sir Stamford snapped at his intercom for the chauffeur to be ready to whisk him away to an equally luxuriant abode back in town. Roger busied himself with making telephone calls and Lou Frescati, deputy MD, groped around for another coffee and a slug of tomato juice. Within minutes this elegantly lit palace was enveloped in darkness as a slow steady stream of big cars started to wind down the drive on their way home. It had been an unusual Sunday. The winners and losers both were glad the ordeal was over.

A session such as the one just ended placed great strain on all involved. Just a few hours sleep and they would all be facing each other again, the machinery of their business about to be re-cast after the Sunday summit and its decisive outcome.

7

Sir Ralph Pinkerton is the UK Chief Executive of Pink Stamps, an offshoot of the American parent company who dominate the trading stamp scene in the USA. Despite all the advantages of past experience and a background of twenty-five years as brand leader back home, they have failed to make any impression on Green in Britain. Their garage accounts are sparser and the shops giving Pink are smaller with much lower turnover than their Green counterparts. They also tend to be in poorer and more often rural areas where heavy stamp promotion is unlikely to be beneficial.

The American Board of Directors have made it plain to their UK team that unless something drastic is done soon to improve the position, the British end of the Pink operation could be wound up. Sir Ralph is aware that the acquisition of an account like Boshko would make all the difference to their survival. It would ensure Pink's future as a viable entity and guarantee the 'big gun' support and commitment from across the Atlantic ultimately to ensure total supremacy.

The Pink Chief knew, however, that the possibility of making such a capture was remote. He had attended symposiums and dinners where Sir Stamford and the Founder were present and noted the rock solid relationship between the two. At least this was his assumption. Now that RB was virtually running things the bond might be less firm and liable to crack. Were Sir Ralph alive to the outcome of yesterday's meeting at the Boshko country retreat he would be in a different frame of mind.

Monday morning and Pinkerton is addressing his generals in the company's considerably less ostentatious premises in the suburbs. It is a worrying time. In a matter of fact way, he outlines the grave picture to his colleagues. The Marketing Manager John Ryman is also present. He knows the problems they face and yet for reasons beyond the rest of the assembly seems less pessimistic than those around him. After the Chief Executive's address, when the ultimatum has been put to the others, there is furious debate among them all. Despite this round the table discussion, no inspiration is forthcoming and the meeting remains gloomy and resigned.

Half an hour later, Ryman coughs quietly and takes the floor. His confident smile is irritating to those around the table, but nonetheless they listen: no-one else has yet made any impact or suggestion to improve things, so there is nothing to lose. The room goes quiet and Ryman speaks.

'One of the problems we've always faced has been lack of information on how Boshko and Green Dragon put their act together. When do they open this store or that? How they think through their promotions and what they do next?'

His audience glared back at him. He was stating the obvious.

'Tell us something new, John,' said Pinkerton. 'Have you found an invisible man who can get stuff out of Bugbear's vaults and lay it in front of us?' The directors smiled tamely, they knew this was a forlorn hope. Ryman went on, his countenance unchanged.

'Recently Boshko and Green Dragon planned a store opening in Scotland aiming to blot out our new Granline supermarket. The idea was to sabotage our inauguration, discredit us in the eyes of the local authorities and launch one of their own. The reason I persuaded Granline to open two weeks early was not because of the Glasgow holiday week, which was just for outside consumption, it was simply because I knew of Bugbear's plans to ruin Granline and accordingly instructed Bob Belper of Granline to open up even if half his shelves were empty and the paint wasn't dry on the trolleys!'

All at once a new atmosphere prevailed. Ryman's cronies were held in rapt attention. The knowledge that at last a Pink Stamp man – John Ryman, had found an 'inside man' in the Green Dragon Empire brought wondering and admiring faces out of the hitherto glum party. Ryman played his audience along – he never mentioned the name of the 'insider' to the assembly. Curiously enough, it didn't seem to matter. They all felt that out of the blue a life-line had appeared: never mind the sordid details which the Marketing Manager must have employed to set it up, that would all come out later. It was time to give thanks.

The astounded Pinkerton put a brake on things. Since appointing Ryman he had given the former Unilever branch manager a free hand to manipulate the Pink sales strategy and promised not to harass him for results too early. Ryman had sworn to his chief that within a couple of years they would be snapping at the heels of Bugbear's band. This was the first real unexpected coup and it took Sir Ralph completely by surprise.

'You've told us all we need to know just now John – we don't want to destroy your excellent plant by blowing the gaff to everyone.' He addressed the others, 'Gentlemen, as you can see this morning looks a lot brighter now than when we came in here. I'm phoning America and putting them in the picture. I'll only say what John has told us. Not only have we got a stay of execution but we might just bury Bugbear after all.'

The meeting closed and the directors poured out. Pinkerton and Ryman were left in the room together. Ryman was offered a cigarette plus a large whisky, while his host waited for the recipient of the drink to continue the conversation. Still Ryman side-stepped the issue of his spy's identity, but what he had to say was more interesting.

'They've set up a sort of command centre,' he started, 'right near the director's level at the top of their HQ. I'm told that one person only has the key to this place, but if we can get our 'insider' to win the confidence of this custodian so that he allows him sight of the material inside, I feel we'll have all the data we need before too long.'

Pinkerton raised his glass, patted Ryman on the back and intimated that if indeed all this could be accomplished a full board appointment with Pink Stamps (UK) would be virtually a formality.

8

The next morning the repercussions of the previous day were not long in coming. Stephen had not been in his office more than half an hour when RB summoned him up alone. It transpired that de Lorean had blasted RB on the phone some twenty minutes earlier but had calmed down when Bugbear promised him an immediate enquiry. As Baxter went in he determined to tell the Chief Executive all the facts – he didn't feel like taking all the blame, why should he? Blame for the sloppiness which accompanied the visit should be apportioned equally. He was ready to defend himself and if need be tell RB what the twelfth floor was really like.

RB's attitude towards Stephen was remarkably calm and without rancour. He must have realised that no one person could be held responsible for all the mishaps that occurred. He certainly was not going to sack Stephen or anything dramatic like that. Despite the fiasco Boshko needed Green Dragon and vice versa, nothing could change their reliance on each other. RB had an idea therefore which should satisfy the client. De Lorean and his henchmen would need some sort of proof that RB had taken action to improve efficiency. As it transpired, the solution, from Baxter's point of view, was a lot less drastic than he had dared imagine.

During the growing years of the Company they had become increasingly involved in the field of sport sponsorship. Starting with swimming, it had expanded to include tennis, riding, athletics and several charities. To take the heat out of the current row Bugbear suggested Stephen should go down to the coast and oversee one of the international tennis tournaments in which the Company had invested £50,000. He could then say to de Lorean that Baxter had been demoted as a reprisal for the poor presentation. Once relations were back to normal he would be quietly reinstated but would be less involved with Boshko.

Stephen felt he had got off lightly and wasn't now inclined to expound his views about the rest of the team. Besides, going off for a while would be a tonic. 'Take Peter Truckley with you.' These last words were the kiss of death as far as Baxter was concerned. While liking Peter he knew only too well how Truckley could quite unintentionally produce disasters out of a hat. Never mind. He had got his reprieve. Better not to argue the toss over the choice of running mate.

Down on the south coast Stephen and Peter were hugely relieved to be out of the Sugar Cube. Both were blissfully unaware of all the decisions and counters being planned in country houses and suburban offices to the north. They checked in to the five star Grand Hotel which was well outside most budget considerations but sanctioned without qualms in this case. In actual fact the job to which they had been ascribed was potentially almost as dangerous as handling de Lorean or those like him – only this time sun-tanned Australians and Americans were the problem. They would be responsible for the smooth running of an event reported daily in the national press. Stephen's prime brief was to co-ordinate the whole show in tune with the local press and radio, while making useful contacts during the hospitality evenings which were held every evening on site. In a sense it was where he had come in. Back then he was truly one of the 'bums', now it was a different ball game!

In their haste to get away from head office the two paroled fugitives inadvertently made a small oversight which would later add to the clouds on the darkening horizon. That was some way off. Right now, sitting in the lounge of the Grand and under the gentle anaesthetic of a few gin and tonics, Baxter felt a world away from the tensions of the past few weeks. He felt secure in the belief that the long tentacles of the Empire would leave him alone in this drowsy dreamland of elderly spinsters and exotic palms. He took in the surroundings – everything seemed unhurried and dignified; a refined, gracious ambiance which was a welcome tonic. The only blight on the horizon to threaten the atmosphere was Peter. Since his resurrection, salvation and subsequent boost in status, Truckley did not see himself under any sort of cloud or the threat of immediate dismissal which loomed clearly for Stephen. Peter had survived incidents guaranteeing an early exit, and yet amazingly was still around. He reckoned now the worst was probably over, and this new jaunt meant he could let his hair down a bit and take in whatever fun and entertainment was on offer.

Whilst Stephen waded through the evening's paper work, phoned newspapers, and organized the late functions, Peter took up the habit of sprawling full length on the deep luxuriant sofa in the lounge, purring over the new set of golf clubs he was breaking in during the day. The manner of their acquisition was a very dubious one. Soon after his unexpected salvation by RB he had decided to celebrate his recovered status by splashing out a bit. He trailed down the road from HQ some 400 yards and sauntered into gift house number one – flagship of the hundred or more spread over the domain. He confidently strode up to the young girl whose job was to check the number of stamps in each book, tear them out and hand over the chosen goodies. These redemption centres were not noted for the high IQ of the staff and so Peter took full advantage. Flashing a five-year loyalty badge, borrowed from a girl-friend in the personnel department, he declared his intention of acquiring a set of golf clubs which would normally require twenty-eight books of stamps for redemption. The new golden boy now played his hand. Despite her limitations the girl facing him was clearly aware that Truckley had nothing like the requisite number of books to make the exchange. She stared hard at Peter's seven books which he laid on the counter. His five year service, he maintained, allowed him the right to merchandise at three-quarters off – or, in this case – seven books would get a twenty-eight book gift. The mesmerised girl had no choice but to hump the clubs over the counter without a murmur.

Baxter had wholly immersed himself in the tennis week. The late evening would find him strung out in the cocktail bar after a day spent wrangling, arguing, pacifying and generally appeasing the immature artisans of the turf.

Friday lunchtime. The week has gone well for despite acrimonious disputes on court and isolated complaints over eating arrangements during the hospitality sessions, no major crisis has arisen. The sun had shone ever since they had arrived and it has only to be dry for Finals day tomorrow for a successful conclusion.

Two young Aussies, unhappy with decisions on court which have led to their exit, followed Stephen back to the Grand, and were on course to wipe out the good feeling which had been a feature of events so far. Stephen was unaware of this as he negotiated the swing door and then dumped his bags at reception. The three of them collided outside the hall porter's lobby. The sponsor's man on the spot saw the likely danger of such a confrontation. A lot of cameramen were also staying at the Grand – a brawl between Green Dragon's envoy and a couple of dissenting players was heaven sent, particularly as they hardly had to leave the bar to cover it all. Baxter had the presence of mind to usher them out of the limelight of main reception to a quiet corner of the huge lounge, shielded by the piano, bass and drums of the tea time orchestra who made gentle music between tea and dinner. He then listened patiently to their grievances in a benevolent mood. It seemed churlish to ban them for thumping a linesman, particularly as they had spent about £500 and had come 12,000 miles for the privilege. Baxter was in a conciliatory mood. He wasn't about to risk a nasty incident when he was so near the winning post. He reinstated them and offered them a liquid lunch in the lounge bar.

It came as no great surprise to find Peter already there, practising his putting on the Chinese carpets. As far as the antipodeans were concerned the change from tent to five-star hotel was overwhelming. The carpets became smeared with wet grass and grit from the soles of their shoes. Two or three retired couples who hitherto were happily chatting in their armchairs beat a hasty retreat. Very quickly the table they had acquired was full of lager bottles at least a couple of which were decapitated when Lenny tried to illustrate his service action to Peter. Baxter was only drinking half measures but his companions made no such concessions as the bottles overspilled the table. Three o'clock and Peter, Lenny and Rod were really getting stuck in. All the guests had gone, and the only company around were the barmen and assistant manager anxiously waiting for them to depart so that they could clean up ready for opening in a couple of hour's time. Peter vanished for a few minutes to reappear with another full crate of beer. One assumed they came from the hotel cellar but at this stage no-one really seemed to care. Four o'clock and the debris of empty bottles, crates, tennis rackets, sweaty towels and golf balls littered the most elegant room in the hotel.

Stephen Baxter looked up from the table. He was in a considerably better state than the others but nevertheless deeply regretted that he had allowed a conciliation drink to develop into such a drawn-out binge. Peering through the aspidistras and palms, he caught sight of a figure in black through the lounge in the telephone recess which adjoined the cocktail bar. Although a glass partition and the swing doors of the lounge were in front, he made out the lean form of the assistant manager. Stephen could swear he was glaring back at him and signalling. The others were very raucous now and becoming unmanageable. He dreaded anyone coming in to find his charges in such a state. The assistant manager pushed the swing doors and poked his head through.

'Mr Baxter, telephone call for you.'

Stephen swallowed hard, grateful that the actual receiver was well out of earshot. He got up quickly, welcoming the chance to distance himself from the others. The assistant manager, however, seemed equally determined to confine his disorderly guests where they were. 'There's an extension on the table next to your friends,' he declared icily.

The man vanished, no doubt satisfied that he had contained the uproar by successfully sealing off the lounge in the way that police officers tape round the area where a murder or major crime has been committed. He did have his own reasons to maintain the status quo. The hotel inspectors were making their annual visit today, and the sight of young men in shorts and sweaty shirts, dropping bottles and horsing around generally would put a question mark on the assistant manager's ability to cope when his superior was away.

Stephen paused before picking up the phone. It had to be head office and probably someone important making sure things were running smoothly. Before he could make a move, Lenny, attempting to balance one beer bottle on another, stretched out and picked up the receiver. Egged on by both Peter and Rod he screamed the first verse of a Sydney street song, finishing with a large burp and allowed his bottles to collapse before throwing the receiver to Stephen.

Dan Turpin was on the other end of the line. He was pretty steamed up before being subjected to Lenny's slobbering, now he was quite beside himself. Whether he cared what company Stephen was keeping seemed irrelevant. He did not bother to ask who was singing as this was something that might well finish everyone.

Dan jabbered like an idiot but the message was clear. The whole Boshko marketing team were to visit the Sugar Cube and attend a meeting in the Op's room in an hour's time. All charts, maps and graphs were set up but where was the Op's room key?

Baxter suddenly felt very sick. He had no answer. With one hand over the mouthpiece he pleaded silence from the revellers to gather his thoughts. On that score he was wasting his time. He visualised the desperate scene on the twelfth floor of the Cube and Dan's predicament – all those hard-headed boys from Boshko standing like lemons outside a locked room while RB, Douglas and Dan flap around ready to pawn their souls for one little key. If ever there was an indictment of incompetence this was surely the conclusive proof. Baxter spontaneously rummaged through his pockets, and suddenly went cold. He pulled out a handful of coins and of course the key! He felt very sick. Whatever happens he couldn't let on to Turpin.

'Sorry Dan I just don't know,' he stammered. It was too late. His frenzied inquisitor had hung up, no doubt ready to consider desperate measures like blasting his way in or making panic calls to locksmiths, or 24-hour 'do anything' outfits. It was now obvious he would have to get out of the hotel and back to the fray as soon as he could. Despite their hazy state the others seemed to grasp the situation and fall in with Stephen's wishes. Someone else would have to come down and handle the finals-day arrangements. Stephen had to go back and try to save his skin.

In the meantime problems had been building up on the other fronts. Both were capable of seriously damaging the hard-won goodwill battle RB and the Founder had waged since the early days. Once again the trouble spots came under Bugbear's banner.

Complaints had been coming in to Vivienne regarding the heavy-handed tactics being employed by the research girls in the field – Annie and Susie. During the incubation period no problems existed. Any feedback coming in from the public was looked on as a bonus. A reasonable number of half-completed questionnaires seemed to be acceptable. The results were therefore disappointing and consequently there were few points gleaned from the streets which the Marketing people could act upon. As other companies in varying fields became increasingly conscious of the value of research, Vivienne was asked to step up both volume of work and more detailed analysis. A quota system was to be introduced – the girls would have to get fifty filled questionnaires per day. Vivienne knew the calibre of her field helpers and doubted whether they could manage it.

Annie was about sixteen stone and from any angle could be taken for an all-in wrestler on parade from the ring. She had a very low IQ and a determined pugnaciousness never to give up on any respondent that might walk away at the wrong moment. The very sight of Annie lumbering towards her prey would be enough to encourage any shopper emerging from a store to give her a wide berth. All in all she was the complete antithesis of what an interviewer should be. That she got the job in the first place was due to Vivienne interviewing her after an agency party and a few too many Martinis.

If Annie represented the heavy brigade, Susie was the lightweight. Matchstick thin after perpetual bouts of overdieting, at least two of her five days interviewing were taken up with visits to dieticians and psychiatrists. Susie tended to confuse her street questioning with her own state of mind and soon became a mental mess. Respondents would feel sorry for her early in a discussion and the interrogator's health grew more important than the interview she was undertaking.

Following the new quota target, Vivienne was most surprised when instead of the usual paltry amount of returns the quantity of questionnaires reaching her desk rose quite dramatically. Closer examination revealed the truth behind the work rate explosion. Beyond 'the multiple advice' section of the form there was left a blank space for the public to give their subjective views on why or why not stamp collecting appealed to them. Scrutinizing the returns Vivienne very soon discovered that most shoppers seemed to say nothing or replied in the same vein. It was obvious the girls had filled in their own forms to make the quota. Vivienne was forced to issue them with an ultimatum – one hundred genuine interviews or they would be shown the door.

It so happened that the first assignment after the warning was to assess shopper reaction to the new French hypermarket just about to open in Caerphilly, South Wales. Such was the importance of the mighty new emporium to the town itself regarding jobs, plus the anticipated flow of business into such a depressed area, that it was natural that there would be an impressive array of dignitaries attending the grand opening. The twinning of the town with its French counterpart brought over the Mayor and Mayoress of Deauville, Monsieur and Madame le Beau. Were they to know what was to befall them, it would have been highly unlikely that they would have made the Channel crossing in the first place.

Sticking to a well-rehearsed plan, Madame le Beau was prevailed upon to make the first purchase, smile at the photographers, and step aside for the genuine shoppers to commence normal trading. This she duly did, but having passed through the check-out, continued to stroll delicately through the exit, clutching a bag of croissants. A naive and fatal mistake. Outside on the tarmac, like starved vultures, the predators were waiting. Helplessly isolated, the stranded female found herself the object of a pincer movement by the quota hungry team. The latter closed in on their prey. The Mayoress, who hardly spoke a word of English, soon withered under Annie's unremitting attack. Little did the unfortunate lady realise that her linguistic incomprehension was interpreted by Annie as a deliberate ploy to frustrate her. No-one had bothered to tell the girls of the opening ceremony and the likelihood of crashing into VIPs.

Suitably peeved by her imposed target, and sickened by the thought that she could well face dozens more pseudo-foreigners acting in a like fashion for the rest of the day, Annie promptly smashed the Mayoress over the head with her clipboard. The elegant visitor, petite and frail at the best of times, just collapsed outright on the concrete, and within a few minutes the unlikely protagonists were surrounded by a crowd of police, ambulancemen and a bevy of highly embarrassed supermarket officials.

The publicity that followed the assault and battery of a foreign visitor was most unwelcome and untimely, but at least it took in the vicinity of a retailing consortium which was highly unlikely to give stamps in the first place. There was no question here of alienating a future client – it merely gave a few smiles to opponents of the system, and reinforced the general impression that those who worked for the stamp companies were thugs and bullies.

Not everyone in the Company was a *News of the World* reader but those who were would invariably turn to page five for the juiciest story of the week. The unlikeliest candidate for such a splash that could be thrown up came from the lower ranks of the Empire. Tom Roshton's job was to supply each and every garage with the currently appropriate signs denoting the number of stamps given with each gallon. He was a bookishly pedantic fellow most unlike his extrovert workmakes and yet commanded much respect from all he came into contact with. He seemed to Stephen a person far too articulate and precise to do such a job – surely he collected fine art and went on archeological digs as well. Somewhere along the line was another string to his bow, and you did not have to be a psychoanalyst to flush it out. All was revealed one Sunday morning in a bout of embarrassing telephone calls.

Roshton's other interest, unbeknown to his colleagues, was as the national organiser of a wife-swapping association. His photograph, on page five of the News of the World, was bad enough to discredit any employer. What made things utterly intolerable was that Roshton had somehow allowed the Company name to be mentioned in the article together with the telephone number.

Weeks after Roshton had been sacked, an amused switchboard was still having to cope with sundry husband and wives, enquiring if the service was still available. Pink stamps took full advantage, and even took on juniors to jam up the Green switchboard on bogus dating enquiries.

Justice was clinically swift in both instances. Both Roshton and the unfortunate Annie were sacked on the spot. Of more immediate concern was the bonanza the tabloid press and the Grocery magazine enjoyed with their respective stories. There was nothing to be done about the Sunday newspaper – it owed its eight million circulation to such revelations, but the trade paper's attitude was a different issue. Obligatory reading for food retailers, it was the weekly bible for new products, personnel changes, store openings and advertising promotions. Most sales were by subscription, ninety per cent of which would be found on product manager's desks. It did not seem, therefore, that with a guaranteed readership coupled to a nominal buying price, there would be any need to 'go sensational' to boost circulation. Gerry Zerola, the proprietor, was a long time enemy of Green Dragon since the day his son broke his leg when his motor bike collided with one of the Company's warehouse juggernauts. Annie's knockdown of the Mayoress was given unprecedented coverage by the magazine. They milked the story for all it was worth. Instead of the staple diet of price rises of food stuffs, cartoons started appearing depicting convoys of heavyweight sales ladies assaulting terrified housewives. After the style of Private Eye, small ads appeared offering spray paint protection from unwelcome inquisitors, all of which were related to the incident. Zerola did his damnedest to blacken the Company wherever he could, and it soon became obvious that unless someone got at him quickly the appalling slant would start to imbed itself into the minds of all the big supermarket chiefs. The task of removing the chip from Zerola's shoulder was down to RB.

It was damage the Company could well have done without. Whether they could survive the ramblings of Boshko or the plans of Pink was a different matter altogether.

9

The anticipation of the return journey to Head Office filled Stephen with dread. There was the certain humiliation among all his colleagues followed by his probable demise. He tried to find some crumb of comfort to alleviate the approaching blow. He could find nothing. Nine o'clock in the morning and they loaded up the van in the forecourt of the hotel. It was raining hard, entirely appropriate thought Stephen. Placards, banners, silver cups, discarded uniforms and badges – all the paraphernalia from the week's jamboree. Overall the week had not been too bad from the sporting standpoint. Despite the mixed weather, TV and radio ensured adequate exposure and the Company name was well plastered on every shop window and billboard in the seaside town.

Peter had spent nearly all his time on the golf course and had turned up just once at the tennis venue, the consequence of which was that Stephen was on call unaided through the days, dolling out lunch vouchers, prizes and liasing with radio stations and the local press. To bear a load like this was tough enough. He didn't feel capable of facing a showdown at the other end of the line on a topic unrelated to his conduct of affairs here.

As the van rumbled out of Eastbourne, he continued seeking solace from any quarter. The noise in the back of the van didn't help. On top of all the equipment, Stephen had reluctantly agreed to take the two Aussies back to Earls Court ready for a tournament at Queen's Club W14. Peter, in fine form, and contrasting markedly from his preoccupied driver and associate, was joking around with the boys in the back, having clambered out of the bench seat he was sharing with his morose companion. It was ten o'clock in the morning and Baxter was already grateful that Peter had not made his presence felt with the tennis crowd earlier in the week. Another distinctive sound joined the rattle, clattering and general melee in the rear. The simultaneous hissing of beer cans being opened. More raucous laughter. Apparently the previous day's session had not made the slightest difference to any of them. Stephen looked in his mirror at the scene behind him. Rod was propped up against the wheel well, a can of Swan in each hand, Larry was sitting on a pile of score pads and Peter nicely wedged between a rolled up tennis net and a ball machine. Had Stephen diverted routes from the A23 to the cross-Channel ferry no-one would have been aware of it. Baxter wished he could change places. Why couldn't he bum around the circuit like them? Fresh air during the day, lagers at night. Perfect.

It was eleven o'clock when they went through Croydon that Stephen brought the transit van to a halt in a layby. Why should he go on brooding when everyone else was having a good time? He was for the chop anyway and a few beers might numb the pain a bit. Indignantly he switched off the ignition, walked round to the back of the van and wrenched open the doors. It so happened that the vibration of the journey so far had shifted the net and Peter to a position where he was leaning on the door; the net providing a comfortable cushion. Truckley crashed onto the road with the net on top of him. He had a nasty crack on the head. He was moaning deeply when the Aussies and Stephen dragged him back into the van from whence he had just come. Baxter's brief flirtation with indignation was over. An emergency. The white van had now become a kind of ambulance minus any sort of qualified helper. He gulped down a couple of beers and wondered what to do next. Depression intensified when he realised the sort of help he could expect from the other two. Rod's solution was to offer Peter another can. It was decided to get the van and occupants back to the Sugar Cube as fast as possible where a first-aid officer could deal with Peter. They took off again at full speed as Peter muttered intermitantly complaining about the improvised headband being too tight. Loose cans swept back and forth on the tin floor as the noise of the debris augmented Peter's cries.

The North London suburbs were now before them. The circumstances now prevailing concerning a horizontal marketing executive lying prostrate behind him would not divert attention from the main billing. Baxter shuddered nervously as he watched the Sugar Cube slowly making its presence felt on the mid-day skyline. Even from almost two miles out he could virtually pick out his office window under the giant 'E'.

They all felt rather sick as he coaxed the makeshift ambulance into the parking bay. He purposely drove right under the building as he had no wish to make a two hundred yard spectacle of four people carrying a body over the tarmac within full sight of the entire edifice. The task of getting Peter out of the van unnoticed was made surprisingly easier by dint of an unexpected diversion. Although his head was still bleeding and he was probably concussed, Peter tottered on his feet supported each side by Rod and Larry. Several policemen were milling around the parking bay area talking to the security men. No-one seemed to know what was going on but it provided enough cover to get all four of them inside without causing a ripple of interest. Stephen deposited the others in the first aid room leaving the Aussies to explain or improvise some explanation. He then braced himself for whatever reception would be in store upstairs. He later remembered this short ascent as being the longest two minutes in his life. The agony prolonged itself when he looked around him. Dan and Laurie were nowhere to be seen. Eugene was drying out somewhere and Falina was at a conference. He poked his head into his own office – at least his desk was still there! So far so good. He gingerly crept round to the Op's room. Female voices emanated from within. It was Vivienne and Gillian, RB's secretary.

'Mr Bugbear, Mr Trossley and Mr Rabbler would like to see you at four o'clock, Stephen.'

Her message passed on, Gillian vanished down the corridor.

'Get another job lined up,' added Vivienne.

Stephen knew all along he was about to be dismissed so both remarks came as no shock. He just wished Vivienne might have been somewhat more charitable. Finally she could tell him everyone else's reaction to last week's episode. Once she was satisfied they were both alone, Vivienne started to fill in the gaps.

'Dan became frantic when he put the phone down on you. We had so little time you see. There was no way into that room without the key. There were eight people involved. RB wanted me on call so if research queries came up I could drop in and clear anything up.'

At this point Stephen prayed that some of the top boys might have been missing. Vivienne named them. 'Sir Stamford, Roger de Lorean, Paul Witner from Boshko. We had RB, Dan, Laurie, Troston and Clive Woods from Haseys.' Stephen waited for her to complete the list but she stopped at eight.

'What about Douglas? I assume he made up the number.'

'I think you're right,' said Vivienne, 'but I'm sure he wasn't waiting outside here with the others.'

Baxter became mortified when she described the scene. It appeared that all of them had queued outside the Op's room while Dan Turpin smashed down the door with an axe.

'Did they go ahead with the meeting?' he asked.

'Yes of course, but not here. After Dan's efforts there were so many slivers of wood, splinters and dust around that RB took them over to the Charcoal restaurant where they hired a reception room. When Sir Stamford saw the size of the Op's room he was quite happy to go elsewhere anyway.'

'What about the others?' asked Baxter.

'It was too much for Dan,' continued Vivienne. 'He's had a kind of breakdown, I hear he's almost incoherent – doesn't seem to know what day it is.'

'And Laurie?'

'He's just relieved it's your problem and not his. RB can't hold him responsible for this. After all it was the MD's idea to send you down on this tennis jaunt. If he hadn't done that we would not have had all this.'

Stephen took his eyes off Vivienne. Ever since he'd come upstairs a policeman had been standing quietly in the corridor, saying nothing.

'Why's he here?'

'He's been on duty here all weekend' she explained. 'Friendly bloke too. I should think he's fed up gazing at the remains of your door!'

'So in actual fact no-one has been inside the Op's room apart from Dan?' queried Stephen.

'No, it's just as you left it before your trip – plus all the mess of course.'

It was still not much past three o'clock. It didn't seem possible a day could pass so slowly. He shook hands with the policeman, introduced himself, and told him his vigil was over. The blue shadow vanished. Stephen wondered how on earth they could spare a man for three days sentry duty. He learnt later that such a posting was not forthcoming without considerable palm-greasing from above. RB had promised the local constabulary unlimited use of the Country Club for their own functions and had thrown in several free gifts from the catalogue for good measure. With all these inducements a more benign and co-operative officer would be hard to find.

Vivienne, anticipating the end of the road for Stephen after his four o'clock rendezvous, invited him back for dinner. He readily accepted and envisaged a sort of timetable for the hours ahead – the misery of losing a job followed by sympathetic compensation from Vivienne.

Both of them started to stroll away from where they were standing when Stephen felt the need to tell her something he had been holding back from everyone.

'Have you asked yourself, why this room has been guarded so zealously Vivienne?' She nodded. They went through the debris back into the Op's room and sat down. Paper, pencils and drinking water were in place, untouched prior to the abortive meeting. The telephone rang. It was Gillian again.

'I'm sorry Stephen, can you make it 5.30 – something's come up.' He put the phone down without making any reply and resumed his explanation of things to Vivienne.

'I think I know why RB is so touchy about this room,' he said. 'Most people are aware that I have all the latest turnover, store openings and budget forecasts of Boshko here.'

Vivienne acknowledged this when Stephen added: 'but there's something else. It may surprise you to know that Boshko are buying up several hotels, pulling them apart, and are planning to give stamps to hotel guests and diners and on all services provided. As you can see this would open up a new dimension in the battle with Pink. They are struggling for existence now. If Boshko and ourselves dominated this new area as well as shops and garages, they would almost certainly throw in the towel.'

Vivienne gaped back open mouthed. No research they had been undertaking had given any clues as to their unpredictable client's intentions.

'It's all partly academic now as far as I am concerned,' he shrugged 'but if Pinkerton's mob knew about this before de Lorean got going for Boshko, they could do something to sabotage the whole scheme – know what I mean – encourage the hotel associations to outlaw it while launching out somewhere themselves.'

Vivienne left quietly, somewhat chastened. She thought she knew what was going on but obviously she did not.

'Be around about eight-ish.'

Vivienne's exit meant Baxter was truly alone. It wasn't a new feeling but one he'd always been conscious of ever since his first day. The lack of windows in the room meant the air was still full of dust and grit. He tied a handkerchief round his mouth and started to make a mental note of the room's contents. Three sides of the room were plastered with charts and pictograms. It was the fourth side or end of the room containing files one to eight that was of any consequence. He knew their position instinctively, and what was in them off by heart. Number one was devoted to Competition. Number two on Hypermarkets right up to Number eight – the file on Boshko's plans which included the hotel project. He seemed relieved that they were all there. He looked a second time and took hold of himself. Counting the black boxes only took him to seven. Where was Number eight? Stephen tried to reassure himself. Perhaps he had taken it upstairs before he went away, or deliberately hidden it somewhere out of view. Despite all the distractions of the past few days he realised this was not the case. Baxter prided himself in the belief that the black boxes appeared so nondescript and accessible that even if an outside party were looking for classified material, they would probably overlook it.

Over the next ten minutes his mind came to terms with the implications of this discovery. Firstly the black box had gone – no question of that. Secondly would this sudden revelation change his fate upstairs in half an hour's time? Doubtful. The die was certainly cast in that direction and no dramatic turn would alter things. He said this over and over again, increasingly surprised by his lack of emphasis. Could he perhaps stun his interrogators by submitting this new evidence? After all his own performance did not ring of treachery, more a kind of cumulative incompetence which had taken an unfortunate turn. Falina, Eugene and Peter in their respective roles were a good deal luckier to be more remote from the scene of power, and hence far less vulnerable than he was. He kept on mulling things over in his mind, trying to justify this and that. He became so pre-occupied with making out a case based on his unexpected 'find', that he suddenly realised that he had completely forgotten about Peter and the others.

The first aid officer seemed irritated with Baxter's belated call. He obviously hadn't relished dealing with Truckley's drinking companions either. They were clearly more trouble than the patient and were apparently unwilling to leave the premises without walking away with the two young nurses who completed the team. Peter, it appeared, would be alright in a couple of days. Of greater concern was the imminent highjacking of female medical staff. Would he come down and sort them out? Baxter looked at his watch. 5.30 pm. Time to go upstairs.

10

The scene in Richard Bugbear's office was just as he had pictured. He had been in this suite so many times it was now as familiar as his own bedroom. There was a difference though. The build up of crises had made its mark on both men and environment. RB was baggy eyed and unshaven, whilst Laurie and Troston were equally disarrayed, the former having probably slept in his suit, and the latter in shirt sleeves and clearly without his contact lenses as he squinted continuously through the smokey air. The Managing Director rose.

'Stephen, as you well know this has been a difficult time for all of us. The problems we face really arise from our own success.' Bugbear then proceeded to ramble on about the growth of the business. It was mostly the same speech when he joined, thought Stephen. The small audience were similarly well acquainted with Bugbear's circuituous route to the point of his argument but were wary of how quickly he could switch back to the issue in hand.

'Whilst we built up several small accounts we were still looking for the big one. When we signed up Boshko in a way our problems were over, and yet automatically they had just begun. We had to offer them such a generous franchise agreement that no grocer of or near that size could trade with stamps closer than a half mile radius. That meant we had to say goodbye to Pipton, Gateman and the Co-op. The Co-op meanwhile started something else, but that's another story.'

Stephen listened intently, anxiously awaiting the moment when the talk would become more personal.

'In those early days the loss of Boshko would have meant that Pipton might have come in and we could have done well enough. We didn't lose them as you know and Boshko are now enormous. Biggest in the country in fact. If they resign – no one is anywhere near big enough to compensate for such a loss. In the last few years we've tripled the staff, overheads, sponsorship and other services to say nothing of the Country Club, executive jet and the rest. In other words, it's a different story now. Apart from the staggering loss of turnover the lack of confidence among our smaller grocers would be ruinous. I'll come to the point Stephen.'

Laurie and Peter leaned forward. They too were familiar with all that had gone before and were now alert to RB's change of tune. 'Your conduct of things in the eyes of Roger, and the little fiasco we've just been through, have both been a disaster. Unfortunately getting you out of the place for a while did not really help since the incident of the smashed door just reinforced the opinion he already had. It gave Roger the chance to back up his case when reporting back to Stamford. To be frank, unless you go I think we'll risk losing them and if that happens this whole Empire which we've built collapses like a pack of cards. We'll give you a month to look around. Laurie and I will be here if you need our advice looking for something else. I'm trying to put it as gently as I can Stephen. If it were up to me and the circumstances weren't so dire I'd never dream of doing this. I'm sorry it had to end this way.'

RB sat down.

'We've no choice' summed up Laurie. 'It's you or everything will fold.'

Stephen felt a kind of relief pass over him. The sentence had been passed. Exactly the verdict he anticipated. He was sure he noticed a smug smile on Laurie's face as the edict was delivered. He said nothing in reply and they probably didn't expect him to. What Boshko knew and the other three didn't was the possibility that through some as yet unsolved piece of espionage Pink Stamps might well have the complete file on the hotel plans to complement their problems.

Bugbear got up a second time.

'In case you're interested you're not the only departing soul around here. DNA left on Friday. Paul Richards has his resignation letter downstairs.'

There was nothing more to be said. It was 6.30 pm and dark outside. They shook hands amicably and for a moment Baxter felt that RB was genuinely sorry about his dismissal.

He grabbed his coat from Gillian who was still in attendance in the outer office, rushed downstairs, jumped in his car and drove off to Vivienne's.

The following morning Baxter got on the phone to Paul Richards, the personnel manager. He liked Paul and although they had had little reason to meet in matters relating to business, Stephen would often meet him at the Country Club for some squash or billiards. They had always had a drink afterwards and got on well together. Paul had been with Green Dragon since its inception and had passed up several other job assignments that had come his way because he felt no other business had such a rich mixture of people and could keep him as involved and interested. The personnel department was a very large one and an impressive team was assembled to process the influx of persons it had to cope with.

They sat down face to face, and Richards learned about Baxter's fate. He was shocked. Although hiring and firing were necessary in certain departments, any such action from either the Board or Marketing Division meant a lot more than either a typist who's always sick, or a driver who's never on time. Richards expected any dismissal from this quarter to have serious reverberations throughout the Company. The issues were likely to be about misappropriation of funds, controlling interests and golden handshakes. Industrial espionage had never been a reason.

Baxter allowed Paul no time to dwell on it. He brought the subject round to Douglas. It was important to find out Richard's reaction to DNA. He need not have worried. The personnel manager shared the general repulsion for Alcott and was quite happy, now that he was gone, to divulge anything about him for whatever reason Stephen possessed. He still couldn't see why Stephen was more preoccupied with DNA's future rather than his own.

'Paul, do you have his resignation letter?' Richards went to his drawer, rummaged through it and found the letter. It was addressed to RB. They sat down to study it.

The gist of the letter to Bugbear was that he needed a new challenge. He felt he had taken the Company a long way and it was time to move on. Details of his new post were quite specific. He was to be the Publicity Director of an American firm in the Mid-West called Crimson Paints. He went on to thank everyone for the 'happy days he'd spent in the Sugar Cube' and signed off in his usual treacly way 'I cherish the happy time spent with you all.'

Baxter handed the letter back to Richards. He then suggested making some coffee as what he had to say might take some time. Once he had made clear to Richards the story of his own dismissal he then added his revelation of the missing file. It was this final point that seemed to stir Richards into action. He made it plain that he would actively assist Stephen in any direction to help solve the mystery.

'Paul, I want you to find out as much as you can about this Crimson concern, I'll be in touch with you if I get anything.'

They shook hands and parted.

The rest of the world meanwhile appeared to be having fun. Surfboards were appearing on the roof racks of mini-cars albeit possessed by owners who would need to go thousands of miles in search of a decent wave. Flowers were adorning everything and if the promised land was 6000 miles in San Francisco the rolling sounds of the new beach culture were lulling its disciples into a world of casual abandonment. Baxter lamented his fate – oh to be a student again – the closeted world of coffees, libraries, sweaters and scarves. It suddenly seemed to be a long time ago.

11

Another part of the field. Or to be strictly precise, the back seat of a limousine. The vehicle is well equipped – mobile telephone, dictating machine and built-in bureau. Every facility for the travelling decision maker. There is but one passenger – John Ryman, the brightest star and the man most likely to shine in the ranks of the Pink Stamp army. He is using Pinkerton's battleship saloon and is tearing back to London from the airport after a ten hour flight from St Louis. He is in a positively happy frame of mind. He has just had the green light from his transatlantic masters on a plan of operation. Although Pinkerton should approve the scheme in a West End hotel in less than an hour's time, Ryman still cannot get there quickly enough. He clears his throat, puts down his drink, and grabs the little tape machine. The other hand presses a button and the glass dividing partition separating him from the chauffeur is raised. His privacy is complete.

'Memo from John Ryman to all senior executives. Subject: hotel penetration mainland UK. Degree of confidentiality – Group Red.'

Ryman pauses and looks around him. The chauffeur is whistling happily and in a world of his own. Quite safe to go on.

'In accordance with intelligence received during the last few weeks, your Company is undertaking the target objective of presenting our stamp plan to hotels in the one to five star category throughout the country. We would have liked more time to prepare this exercise but we know the opposition is poised to do this very thing. A two per cent penetration and strike rate should be aimed for. The schedule will run as follows:

Week one. A signed letter from Sir Ralph will reach the Managing Directors of all five major hotel groups.

Week two. Hotel managers across the land will be invited to seminars under the control of training managers.

Week three. Special stamp terms to be negotiated for conference as opposed to private hotel clients. . . .'

There was a click and the wheel on the tape machine went wild. The tape had broken. Ryman cursed, tapped the partition and urged the driver to step on it. He threw himself back in the seat and poured another drink. 'Not long now', he thought. The coup of coups was about to be launched. Before the day was out Pink would be all set to embark upon a venture that was sure to reverse the stamp trend in Britain. No longer would they play second fiddle to Green. It would be like Pepsi overtaking Coke or Christie's dumping Sotheby's. The marketing turn around of the decade with John Ryman as the linchpin. He sank deeper with a self-satisfied smugness as his black charger approached the metropolis.

12

Baxter felt himself in a state of limbo. He was neither employed nor unemployed, his work was finished, yet unfinished. Of one thing he was sure. He must try and fathom out how the file got out of the Op's room. Once that was done he would be in the right frame of mind to think about a fresh start in a different field. The atmosphere in the Sugar Cube had become far too claustrophobic to permit any such musings to take root. The Three Horseshoes pub, a pint of beer, and a seat in the beer garden would be the right setting. The lack of distractions in the gentle ambiance of the village inn did nothing to aid his concentration however. He had a mental picture of that nightmare lunch with DNA. After an interminable meal, during which time it was a case of perpetually parrying questions from the publicity manager, they had come back to HQ where Alcott was fleetingly shown the layout and contents of the room. Anticipating DNA's curiosity, Stephen had warned Vivienne that should they come back and see the nerve centre together she was to break in and make an excuse for Baxter to lock up the room and leave. This actually happened and Alcott was given the barest opportunity of remembering any location of this or that before being ushered out.

Over and over Baxter played and replayed that day's events as best he could. He was quite positive also that the last day, and indeed time, anyone had been inside up to Dan's break-in, was that perfunctory inspection so well cut short by Vivienne's intervention.

It was almost lunchtime closing, and several beers later when he had the answer. How had he been so careless? Such was his hurry to get Douglas out he had obviously slammed the Op's room door without locking it. Alcott must have realised this and tried his luck sometime later during the day when he knew few people would still be around. Stephen faced up to the realities. DNA returned unseen, turned the knob and walked in. Too easy to be true. Dan, therefore, had had no need to break the door down – it was unlocked throughout Stephen's absence. He felt ashamed when he realised the impact of this little slip and its terrible effect on Dan.

Each one of the main characters were now facing their own kind of Waterloo. They seemed to be equally divided between those in a great hurry to achieve something and those desperately anxious to sustain and preserve their own position.

De Lorean was hell bent for dispensing with Green Dragon, Sir Stamford was for staying put. John Ryman acting on his leak, was feverishly executing his own plan both to put his own name in lights and in the process simultaneously saving Pink and decimating Green. Stephen, for his part, was determined to put the record straight, and if he could save his own job in so doing, so much the better. RB was very worried, he knew how delicate things were with Boshko – if his staff kept on appearing incompetent he could come a cropper himself, and his comfortable lifestyle vanish overnight. He was never popular with the other directors on account of his rare and superior airs, plus the fact that marketing had become such an intangible factor, wasting thousands with nothing to see for such a great outlay of persons and material. Peter Truckley was fortunate his own misdemeanours occurred at a time of great activity elsewhere. If he could keep a very low profile he would survive, always assuming the Company did.

The minor players were also not without their problems. Dan Turpin's wife held Baxter responsible for her husband's breakdown – if she could get back at him in some way, she would. Laurie had pinned his star to RB and was everywhere identified as the MD's shadow. His own protection would depend upon the guaranteed ejections of both Stephen and de Lorean from their respective places. If this could be so arranged he was still a viable person. Troston would be an immediate goner if Boshko went. The system would still tick over on the small accounts for a while, but those whose jobs were solely tied up with the big retailer would be out of the door in five minutes.

Falina and Eugene were both in when Stephen got back to his office. They had come out of their respective shells and preoccupation with personal matters, to be fairly aware of what was going on. They understood that Baxter was threatened but had no idea that his term had but four weeks to run. There seemed no point in telling them and thereby set off a general panic.

Eugene was entertaining one of his bookmaker friends and Falina was struggling with a translation from a recent conference when Stephen's phone rang. It was Paul Richards.

'I've got something for you Stephen. Can you come down right away?'

He didn't need much encouragement. He was with Paul in a couple of minutes. The personnel manager's desk was covered by a couple of large maps. Richard's girl brought over two coffees as both men pored over the table. Both maps were of the USA one large scale and the other small. Richards ignored the general map, picked up a ruler, and concentrated on the detailed one. It covered the densely populated area of the Mid-West South of Chicago.

'Crimson paints are based in Alton, Illinois. When I found out that from the US Chamber of Commerce frankly it didn't mean much. I naturally then checked out the head office of Pink stamps.'

'Where's that Paul?' interrupted Stephen enthusiastically. 'St Louis, Missouri' was Richard's flat reply.

'No real connection then. Nice try Paul.'

'Listen Stephen, that was my reaction until I took a closer look.' Richards had ringed both locations. Stephen began to perk up again.

'St Louis is on the border with Illinois. Alton the first town in Illinois. The latter is merely an appendage of the big city no more remote than an outer suburb. Both places are therefore virtually one and the same.' The investigators rose simultaneously and smiled at each other, their case proven. It was now up to them to present their case to Messrs Bugbear, Rabbler and Troston. There were still a couple of snags to overcome which could prevent a successful outcome. Firstly there was no factual evidence to show it was DNA who had taken the file. Stephen had never told RB or the top boys about DNA's daily interest in his work or their furtive lunch together. The only move to support such an accusation would be DNA's sudden resignation or as Richards and Baxter would testify – his defection.

The second aspect was that regardless of how the file vanished the responsibility was still Stephen's. RB was still unaware of the burglary.

Despite the ramifications Stephen decided to seek an immediate audience with RB. With Richards' approval he picked up the receiver and spoke to Gillian.

'I'm sorry Mr Baxter. There's a bit of a panic on. Mr Bugbear and Mr Rabbler left for Boshko HQ about ten minutes ago. I'll tell him the moment he returns that you want to see him.'

Stephen shrugged his shoulders then thanked Paul for all his efforts. There was nothing left to do. He went upstairs again and kicked his heels. The day passed slowly and there was still no call from Gillian. He couldn't stand the hanging around any longer. May as well go home and brood on it there. He'd just bought a flat on the edge of the Green Belt and much needed doing to it. Wielding a paint brush would be good therapy to fill in a few hours, and if anything happened Richards would ring him. Stephen picked up his paper and as he was closing his window noticed Peter Troston's Ford Granada swinging into the compound. He would almost certainly know why RB was so long detained. Stephen aimed to catch him as he came into the building. They ran into each other in the parking bay. Troston looked terrible. He had heavy bags under his eyes, his tie was hanging loosely around his open neck shirt and his suit looked as smart as a crumpled crisp packet. It was nothing like the man Baxter was used to seeing. He dropped some papers from his hand but made no effort to recover them in the rising wind. He came over to Baxter.

'It's gone, Stephen, finished for good. After all these years. What am I going to do? You're OK you'll get something, but it won't be that easy for us.'

Troston paused, then uttered the words that everyone in the Green Dragon Empire hoped would never be heard.

'Boshko have just fired us. I've just come back. RB and Laurie were practically thrown out of the place. When the press gets this one we'll have no chance. They've been waiting for this for years. If I were you Stephen, I'd just pack your bags and leave. De Lorean called us over and made the announcement. RB's face was pink. Sir Stamford avoided looking at him throughout. This was never the way he wanted things to go. I think he's taken it almost as badly. The end of an era, Stephen, the end of an era.'

The alarm bells could be heard echoing around the Sugar Cube. To Stephen at this juncture they seemed entirely appropriate. It reminded him of one of those science fiction or Bond pictures, where the villian's hideout had been located and surrounded and there he was, desperate to escape, all his henchmen having been eliminated and everything closing in on him. Once again he shuffled together the events and circumstances which had brought him to the state of affairs he was now contemplating.

Boshko had gone and in no small way due to his own negligence. Granline would not take up the franchise and there was no other food retailer of significant size to plug the gap and thus maintain the Empire's £60 million turnover tag. Sponsorship would cease automatically and every tennis player or swimmer doing his bit would have to switch from closeted hotel to camping in a field. The ramifications following the loss of Boshko would be far reaching and affect the shopping scene nationwide. One would not have to be particularly perceptive to see this news triggering off a domino effect with the other pieces going down very quickly. Fifteen years of building up the whole system could conceivably evaporate in fifteen months, and it could be much less. There was no way of knowing since there was no precedent to go by.

And who would have most to lose from the breakup of the Empire? It was, after all, a private company still – the Founder held practically all the shares whilst his young wife, RB, and the remainder of the board, the balance. The Empire would shed its five-thousand but what about those other thousands indirectly locked in and relying on the system for their livelihood?

Stephen stopped the day-dreaming and came to his senses. There was still no trace of anyone within earshot or indeed anywhere on the floor at all. He rifled through his desk – three years of reports, memos, ideas – what was worth taking? He emptied out all the drawers. It was amazing that this offering of inconsequential papers was the sole testimony to his being around. It seemed so inadequate for a cause that had so impinged itself on his lifestyle to the detriment of a would-have-been social existence. He rapidly unpinned the photographs and momentos from the cork board above his desk, winning and presenting cups, the piece in the newsletter when he arrived, the experimental Big 50 stamp, flattering testimonial letters from children who saved three years for a bike; offers, threats and promises from retailers who would not play the game.

The priority was now just to get out and wash away the memory of the last few days. All matters relating to his pay off and severence could be cleared up wth Paul Richards in a month or so's time after a holiday somewhere. The silence on the floor was unnerving. The distant sound of shattering glass echoed up from Stephen's open window. Baxter retraced his steps and peered down below. The 'E' beneath which he had been ensconced for his period of tenure was now in thousands of pieces. The engineers, whether by neglect or premonition, had allowed the illuminated sign to burn unchecked for almost a week and the build up of heat had taken its natural toll. The first generation tower block all at once seemed to be exposing its warts and boils – any chance of Baxter symbolically slamming his office door for the last time was thwarted as its sandwich layered base met resistance from a racked up floor tile on the uneven composition floor. Nothing else seemed to matter as much as making his exit without encountering anyone. He felt like a jewel thief in the early hours of the morning, terrified of being apprehended. So far, so good; out of the room and swiftly down the passage. Two empty lifts beckoned. No, thank you: he'd take the stairs. Images of someone flipping the power switch with him inside did not appeal. How many times had that happened in a late night film! Clutching the memorabilia about him, the dash earthwards began. Relief was two minutes away. In that time he would be out of the Sugar Cube for ever. Twelve, eleven, ten, nine, eight. Two thirds of the way down – no other noises except the resounding clutter of his furious sprint. The gold fountain pen in his inside suit pocket, unused to his kind of pace, ejected itself on the seventh floor, shooting out at a tangent along the passage whilst Stephen hurtled on. Second thoughts: he couldn't just leave it. He scurried back up to recover it, then froze in his tracks. Far off voices. Stranded now between floors six and seven he guessed the sound emanated from about three levels below. They were becoming discernably louder. Work, brain, work. A dignified descent would have to be the best option but now a somewhat stupid move since whoever was on the way up could not have failed to speculate about what on earth was belting down on them at such a frenzied rate. He dismissed hiding away in the labyrinth of corridors despite the ample cover they provided. He looked around. The aliens were but two levels below him. He made out two male voices and their conversation was clearly audible. Neither could claim allegiance to the English Speaking Union or the Royal Shakespeare Company.

'Everything must be turned over, Phil; from what they say the twelfth and thirteenth are the likely hiding places.'

Stephen was plain scared. He had nothing to do with any malpractice. He was the original pawn, with nothing to show for all his anxiety and worry of the past few months. He needed salvation and preferably within about ten seconds. He found it without moving: the sixth floor toilet. He dashed inside. There were at least eight empty cubicles. Sprinting up to the one furthest from the entrance he rammed the 'engaged' sign across the lock. God, no! How stupid, thought Stephen, if they come in and look along the line of doors the 'occupied' sign will betray him instantly. He reverted to 'vacant', leaving the door almost closed so as to hide himself and clambered on to the toilet seat and waited, praying that the investigators, whoever they were, would go on up to the top and he could make his escape. A sudden blast of cold air confirmed the worst, Stephen shuddered as the CID burst in with the dignity of a pair of bull elephants discovering a lost waterhole. Resigned to his immediate apprehension, Baxter hardly moved. A momentary delay perhaps, or were they preparing to persuade him to surrender peacefully? The answer was swift and noisy. Simultaneous calls of nature, not closing in on the suspect, were the order of the moment. Ablutions complete, both officers withdrew their hands from the washbasins and faced the glass. A continuous mirror flanked the washing facilities. Stephen followed their movements through a small crack in the side of the door. He was less than six feet from the running water. His freedom seemed irrevocably lost as he remembered the old James Cagney movie where the gangster got himself trapped by climbing up a tower and coming to a dead end. This position offered little improvement to that of the Hollywood star except perhaps Stephen wouldn't be shot. One of the men wore a dark blue suit, regulation striped shirt, short hair cut, fair hair, he was thirtyish; his companion was older, stockier, wearing a slate grey suit, he was grim, anxious to wind things up. He was calling the shots.

'It seems like he used a few bit-part actors as well, Phil. Oh yes, by the way there's a library up there. Don't be too long. I want you to help me go through the offices.'

'Aren't we a bit late, Frank? There's not much left to chew on. Anyway, it's this Bugbear character we need.'

The senior officer bit his lip. 'Phil, we are still looking for him.' Exasperation and agitation were written all over his face.

Baxter was uncomfortable now and was conscious of every exhalation of his own breath. He couldn't afford to rest, he was even holding on to the toilet floor – the slightest sound or reflected shadow would give him away. Why the hell don't they go? Both officers were combing their hair. Words were in short supply. Without warning the water pipes which circumvented the rear of the toilets came alive in a crescendo of fury. The roaring din provided Stephen with a chance to drop his guard. A sign of relief as he lodged everything on the cistern. He could feel some circulation come back into his arms. The luxury of a discreet cough could even be indulged. The Niagara flood obliterated everything. In less than a minute the gurgling and belching of the cistern died away. Stephen reverted to his disciplined silence. Blessed deliverance! No voices or shuffling from outside. He could see the mirror – no reflections. The men had gone. Baxter edged out warily, his heart still pounding erratically. He paused momentarily to wonder whether a career of selling soap at Lever's or buried on a production line at Vauxhall's Luton might not have been a safer and less stressful experience. If he managed to extricate himself from this mess without landing in police custody, that would be an achievement in itself. Any higher aspirations were fanciful and quixotic. What employer would give even the time of day to someone whose immediate form guide has been primarily a protracted course in industrial espionage, supplemented by less well-rehearsed activities such as hiding in lavatories to avoid police detection? With this sort of background, perhaps the eclectic tastes of a Foreign Legion recruitment sergeant might take him on. And there was always the Navy. Stephen perked up. A renaissance of spirit was discernable. He started to feel better, only coming down a few points when he remembered how distinctly unwell he'd become half an hour after piloting a boat on the Serpentine. What about a reference? Not so easy. Every connection with Green Dragon must be disclaimed. If Stalin could write off millions of lives and years in the 30s, surely he could cover up his recent past. He'd concoct something pretty conventional with no traces or comebacks – an off-licence assistant in Cornwall or a tenant farmer from Scotland. So long as the place was remote and the occupation believable. But there remained the little question of the reference. He could sink to basics. Gentle bribery. Disbursement of the silverware he had could illicit instant commendations from whomsoever he chose.

Outside at last. Freedom. He ran his eyes up and down the High Street. An inclination to borrow a time machine and push the lever back twenty years. The Escorts and Cortinas have vanished, there are no yellow lines and no Boeings up above. Click. A much quieter scene. Scarcely half the people around. Browns, greys, olive green. A Vickers

Viscount threads through the sky and those who are around gaze up in wonderment towards an uncrowded sky. A Standard Vanguard and a Morris Minor struggle bravely up the road; both are shiny black and come to a sedate halt outside the cinema. The crowd in their drab hues are gawking fondly at the newly sited hoardings – Stewart Grainger for the whole week plus a newsreel and a cartoon. The faces of the eager onlookers are a pasty white. No foreign faces or the prospect of any greater expedition save the two weeks in Margate in a Spartan guest house for the conservative, or the holiday camp for the more lively.

Click. The spell is broken. Something motionless yet familiar was distinguishable on the kerbside. Eugene was sitting on the pavement. He wore a blank vacant expression and was staring with a fixed bewildered gaze across the road. The sort of look that perhaps a long-encarcerated crocodile in a zoo pool would present after decades of inaction. The temptation for onlookers was to throw a penny just to make him blink. None of the afternoon shoppers were paying him the slightest attention. He was squatting precariously close to the traffic, nonchalantly manipulating two pieces of dried-up chewing gum down a manhole cover, with his foot. He broke into a smile on Stephen's approach. Baxter noted his lips moving, but a huge articulated lorry drowned Eugene's voice. Undeterred, the Irishman repeated himself.

'I'm going to be with the Tube, Stephen. From now on, it's up and down London all day long. The early shift starts at 5 am and ends at 2 pm – lots of spare time! If I can't drive them well enough after training, my father has a little shop in Wexford where he'll be selling the Waterford and the like. Seems like going to confession has come up trumps. I even won at Haydock yesterday!'

Baxter tried to hide the incredulity he felt. The last person on earth who should be let loose driving a crowded underground train had to be Eugene. With his record of driving offences, including two proven instances of falling asleep at the wheel, the future consequences of his change were indeed dire. Baxter felt it was his duty to avoid ever using London Transport again.

'Sounds wonderful, Eugene.'

A long silence was followed by the realisation that O'Hara would willingly shunt a busy Tube train for half a hour in a siding if it meant the chance to dissect the day's race card in a proper fashion. It was time to dismiss these little criticisms. At least Eugene had come up with a job, even if his tenure in the position was destined to be of an attenuated duration. What of the others? Those four thousand souls plucked out of the air to fulfil a promise and purpose no longer needed. Who would take them in? Had Falina, Eugene and the rest acquired some sixth sense, found out about the Boshko decision, and taken flight accordingly? If so, he didn't understand how, or he'd nailed Peter Troston less than an hour after the big showdown. It frankly didn't matter anymore. He'd remembered times when the place was deserted for no reason at all.

The next thing he remembered was waiting for a bus less than half a mile from his erstwhile office. One went to London, the other up to St Albans. Either route was acceptable. Stephen felt that out of the stifling atmosphere of political in-fighting he would have a chance to breathe.

With a good few hours remaining before the onset of the rush hour, the 621 was virtually empty. Two passengers were in the top deck – a generously proportioned housewife at the front and a man at the back. A lifetime of acute queasiness when travelling in the rear determined his forward position, opposite the lady. An enormous pile of shopping occupied the remainder of the seat. He could hear his heart thumping in protest at the kind of treatment it had endured during the last few hours, as the lady commenced chomping her way through a ham sandwich, the whole motion punctuated by a consumptive smoker's cough. Not the kind of company to be saddled with on a crowded vehicle or a transatlantic flight, thought Stephen, as he turned his eyes upward toward the small ads which ran around the interior of the roof. One warned of the dangers of acne and its prevention; the other the £50 for failing to pay the fare. Most prominent was a card recruiting potential drivers, proclaiming similar advantages to those about to be offered to Eugene as a Tube operator. 'Ah well,' mused Baxter as he squinted over the small print of the recruitment blurb, 'here at least was a last resort. The throbbing engine was having the effect of a minor earthquake – most of the lady's snack was disintegrating into crumbs and her Boshko-emblazoned carrier bag was losing the battle to contain a split box of washing powder and some over-ripe grapes. Notwithstanding this little distraction, Baxter wondered why he was not feeling completely relaxed and emancipated. There were no grounds for any further worry. He was away and free and every second that much more distant from the hated white building which had become the emblem of his distress. The logic was plain enough but something wasn't quite right. A nagging doubt was still gnawing away at him. He suddenly felt very cold. The sort of feeling that comes with a stroll in a deserted graveyard, regardless of the hour. The cause of this uneasiness was located about twenty feet from his person. The figure at the back. He couldn't look around, or he was finished; but the warning lights were on. Baxter tried to piece together the split seconds before he sat down. The very shape of the man – it had to be Bugbear! Baxter stared ahead, petrified. What could he do if it was RB? All at once the parts of the puzzle assembled themselves in his mind. The erstwhile managing director had taken the least obvious escape route. Stephen braced himself for a confrontation. Perhaps he knew a way out; a hastily-concocted pact to enable this high flyer of yesterday a free passage to obscurity in return for his own unencumbered escape to a less nervous life. Such was his total concentration Baxter failed to notice the absence of the lady opposite. It was time to face the man who until sometime earlier had been the power behind the throne. He swung around. A tramp was occupying the back seat. No RB, no fugitives, no one who could pose a threat to anyone.

It was 3 o'clock in the afternoon. The sun was shining. He felt better already. A news-stand nearby had some lunchtime editions of the Standard. Perfect. Just what he needed, thought Stephen. Racing, sport, films – ignore the business news and relax a bit. He handed over 20p, and just for good measure a full book of saver stamps.

'There you are. I hope it gives you more pleasure than it gave me.'

The vendor showed his appreciation by ripping open a new batch of later editions from the roll and giving Stephen the Late Extra. Just at that moment a bus drew up. He jumped aboard and climbed upstairs without even bothering to see where it was heading. He slumped down and opened the paper. The headlines concerned 'Fresh arms controls' so he flipped to the sport on the back page. As he turned the newspaper over his eyes ran over the STOP PRESS section below the football news and crossword.

The letters were in bold type – **'TRADING STAMP SHOCK'**. Stephen's astonishment was at once overlapped by extreme frustration. In his anxiety to give out the new edition the newsboy had torn off the outside edge of the paper. Only those three words were left. It was akin to a dying man revealing the name of his murderer but expiring after the words, 'it was'. . . .

All thoughts about going away were long gone. He had to satisfy his curiosity and grab the last edition. Only then could he vanish from the scene peacefully and give all his attention to making a new start. The word 'shock' could mean anything. He remembered how the mid-morning billboards would apply the word to anything. It was almost always an exaggeration 'Trevor Francis shock' turned out later on in the day to be nothing more serious than that the footballer had a bruised ankle. Provided he had not been stripped of all his power, or too seriously weakened by de Lorean and his bully boys, Sir Stamford would have done the decent thing and promised not to release the story for at least three days. This would at least enable the Founder to be flown in and convene the other directors so that they could prepare a statement which would present a united front to the outside world. This way the Company might not be written off overnight and the slim chance of finding a replacement would not be jeopardised. The 'doves' of Boshko were for an amicable parting, de Lorean's hawks for a stormy divorce.

Stephen had sprung off the bus totally incognisant of where he was or what to do next. Whilst one half told him to forget everything about the business since whatever announcement was made could no longer affect him, the other half burned with understandable curiosity. The latter prevailed. He would go home, plant himself by the radio, learn the news, and then concentrate on fixing a holiday and his own future.

As it turned out he had decanted himself rather well, just a ten minute stroll from the small flat he bought when taking up the original job offer. The walk through the park threw up fresh scenarios. Perhaps the government were threatening to ban stamp trading, a move some MPs had wanted for years. Was it a revelation about Pink? Could they be winding down here leaving a clear field for Green and Co-op Blue?

He turned the key in the door, hung up his coat and made himself some tea. It was ten to four. He switched on the radio and fiddled with the tuning dial until some light orchestral music signified the right station. Nothing to do now except sip his tea and wait for the four o'clock pips. The music gently evaporated and in came the announcer.

'It's four o'clock and here are the main points of the news. In North West India fighting is still continuing in the disputed border country just south of Kashmir. Government officials say the rebels are putting up stiff resistance but the arrival of fresh troops from Delhi should help to ensure a ceasefire before the end of the week.

Back home, a major change in British retailing is heralded by an announcement broadcast at lunchtime today. The Green Dragon organisation, pioneers of stamp trading in the UK, are to close down their current operation in favour of discount stores. The system, brought over from the USA in the early sixties, is failing because shoppers prefer cheap prices to stamps. It is feared there will be many redundancies. Mystery surrounds the whereabouts of erstwhile Managing Director, Richard Bugbear. Our home affairs correspondent called at their offices today and was told by a spokesman that their Chief Executive was on holiday in the American Mid-West for an unspecified period. We will bring you news of any developments as they occur.

Today's weather, bright and sunny, with occasional showers coming in. . . .